KNOTTED

TAILS OF DOMINANT DESIRES

VOL. II

RED
FERRET
PRESS

Knotted
Volume II

EDITOR-IN-CHIEF: Weasel
EDITOR: Jonathan W. Thurston
PROOFREADER: Sendokidu Adomi

Copyright © 2018 Red Ferret Press

ISBN: 978-1-948712-05-7

Cover by TabaxiTaxi

Printed in the U.S.A.

If you would like a copy of Knotted, you can order one from the online store at Red Ferret Press.

Red Ferret Press
Manvel, TX
An Imprint of Weasel Press
http://www.redferretpress.com

TABLE OF CONTENTS

Jesus died for somebody's sins, but not mine.
-Patti Smith, Gloria

It's out. Finally right? I mean, I've only been workin' on this for like fuckin' forever! This is a beast not easily satisfied. With all the missteps taken along the way, I'm happy to be able to present this one last volume of Knotted, a collection of kink related stories to feed the desires of our readers.

Hunger is an ocean, a dominating void only filled when it gets what it wants, and Knotted is the buffet sitting right outside of the gym. It's temptation, inviting you to enter it's doors and fulfill your wildest curiosities.

So light up a cigarette. Pour yourself whatever mid-shelf drink you like, and take a dive into this cavern of darker pleasures. We all have to get our fix.

KNOTTED

AN OBJECT LESSON
RECHAN

"You can do this," I said to my reflection in the sun visor mirror. "You're tough. This is way less scary than what you've already been through." Then why did it feel like I'd stuck my tail in a garbage disposal and someone's finger hovered right over the switch?

The mantra hadn't helped the last two times I'd said it, but looking at the dash clock I knew it was time. I climbed out of the car, and with a deep breath, passed through the café's front door.

Going through was tough. Not through the doors. Sure, the scent of coffee punched me square in the nose and I had to hold my muzzle up and breathe through my mouth until I wasn't disoriented, but I wasn't as nervous just then. Everyone inside knew how canines were, and hopefully nobody gave the floundering wolf any dirty looks while I hung out by the door. No, I didn't start floundering until I saw the doors out to the café's patio, but after a deep breath and a pep talk, I blew right through 'em.

Once past the doors, it didn't take me long to spot what had me in knots. She sat by the water fountain.

She wasn't what I was expecting.

Even though the pics on her site hadn't shown her head, I wasn't surprised she was a raccoon. No, what caught me were the big earring, multiple colorful bangles, and a purple peasant's blouse; she looked like someone's favorite aunt. The settling twilight made the colors pop amid her darker markings, especially her hazel eyes. The smile she showed when she spotted me was as bright and welcoming as the rest of her. She waved, and I couldn't help but return both smile and gesture.

When I reached her table, she stood and extended her arm. "Hi. I'm Piper."

Mirroring the gesture, we politely sniffed each other's wrists. My nose had finally recovered from the sandblasting it had received inside, allowing me to pick up the natural scent of raccoon, and above that were the vibrant smell of spring grass and loamy earth. "James, but to most people I'm Spades."

Her eyes shone with a vibrant curiosity. "Spades?"

"I play a lot of poker, plus the black fur."

"Surprised no one calls you Jack."

If I had a dime for every time... "A little too on the nose, I guess."

She sat, and so did I. As soon as I did, she quirked her head.

Did I just mess up?

Guess she read my mind. "It's interesting you sat without asking permission, or if I minded."

Aw shit. "Sorry, sorry. We set to meet, I assume--"

"No, no, it's cool." She touched my forearm and smiled. "That's what normal people do. And dominant people. But when a submissive meets me for the first time, sometimes they're deferring to me before we've established anything, even in a public meet'n'greet like this. Either natural tendency or they're hyper-conscious of it." Piper talked with her hands, a typical raccoon thing, and the tinkle-rustle-click of her bracelets gave an odd counterpoint to her voice.

She didn't seem too perturbed talking about this openly in public, but then she wouldn't have invited me here if she wasn't, but I still leaned forward and lowered my voice. "Well... I've only ever really done that sort've thing in the bedroom. Under real specific rules, and I wasn't..." Finding the words was like playing darts in the dark.

Piper's muzzle curled into that good smile, and she mirrored my quieter tone. "You've done this before then, okay. That makes this a little easier. Clair—ah, Dr. Shapiro didn't tell me a whole lot about you."

"What did she tell you?" My ears flicked forward, and I held my breath.

"There was someone she thought I might be able to help, who might benefit from what I do, I might like you, and it wouldn't be a sexual thing. Couldn't go into details about what the issue was, I'd need to hear it from you. What'd she tell you about me?"

Muscles unclenched. "A link to your site so I could email you, mentioned you used to be a pro-dominatrix."

She mmhm'd. "Not much to go on, then. Great, we'll start fresh. What brings you to me?"

"Well I... well, why'd you quit spanking people professionally?" Dammit, why did I not do this over email? Because I dwelled on it even more in front of the blank screen, wrestling with every line. I realized I'd not even paid attention to the answer. "Sorry, uh—"

"James." That held me up. She pinched an empty cup and wiggled it toward me. "I'm thinking I'd like another. Can I get you anything while I'm inside?"

"Braver than me, I don't want to go back in there with that scent." I pulled a face, she laughed. "Just a water, thanks."

While she was gone I stared at the ground in her absence, tracing the lattice of the metal table with a fingerpad. Cards on the table, man. Ripping band-aids and all that. For the five hundredth time I wished she hadn't insisted on a public meet, settled for a phone call instead. Ruminating – that's the word Shapiro used – had me until I heard her clacky shoes come back through the doors.

"I'm impotent."

Piper halted, the water held half-way toward me. After she recovered and offered, I took the bottle. "Thanks," I said, uncapping it and taking a hard pull.

"Ah." She sat down. "Spades, are you okay talking about this in public?"

I glanced down, finding Piper's eyes and ears intent on me. The outdoor area was mostly deserted, except for a hare plugging away on a laptop across the patio, a couple of college kids giggling over their textbooks and phones. "I've been telling you all this so far."

"Alright. Well, that explains a few things. What're you looking for then?"

Rubbing my thighs and twitching my tail didn't help the restlessness. "Looking for ways to be intimate without being sexual. The doc says satisfying a woman is important to my ego, finding another way to be pleasing and supportive in a romantic relationship. Not to mention something I'd enjoy doing, too."

Before she could speak, I cut in, "And I know you're thinking 'you could just go down on a partner', but then it feels like I'm looking through glass at something I can't have, that I'm being taunted with it."

"I get it." Her words were soft, her eyes too sympathetic.

Looking at her face started to make my stomach up tense up worse, so I focused on a plant above her head. "This is what me and Dr. Shapiro go over. And no, before you ask, drugs don't help. I got diagnosed with... ehh, you don't want the long and messy details. Let's just say complications, and even the meds that do work, it's back to having it rubbed in my face again."

"I'm guessing you're not the poly type, either? Not comfortable letting someone else take care of that?"

"Jackpot," I said. "You see my problem." Even though I still didn't look at her, I relaxed a little in the chair. Now it was all out there, and so far no sympathy party, no coddling.

"That sounds like all the usual answers. So let's start talking about kinky stuff. Just checking in." She splayed her hands, bangles jingling. "Rather than start with the specifics, I'd like to hear why you were interested in BDSM before all this happened. What did you get out of it?"

After sitting back and thinking about that a minute, I said, "Aside from the purely sexual component, I liked giving. It wasn't fun to do something just because I was told to, but orders were direct, I knew what and how she wanted something done without second guessing. It felt like the whole world was just me and her, and I existed to make sure she was pleased. And once she was satisfied with me, she'd reward me with what I like the

5

way I liked it."

Piper's bright eyes studied me. "And now that you can't get what you like?"

I sighed and spread my hands. "That's why I'm here. Looking to try."

A smile. "Good." Mischief twinkled in her eyes. "I have an idea or two, then. First though, just to make sure, bondage and pain aren't your thing either?"

I shook my head. "Not really."

"Guess it can't be that easy, huh? Well, I've got something in mind we can try. But that should be somewhere more private." Fishing her phone out of her purse, she tapped it and the glow lit up her features. "Your number?"

All that anxiety and now my whole body unclenched. She was okay with it. We swapped numbers, and I had braved the whole thing.

I swung by her place that Saturday. Oddly she specified during the day, close to dusk––usually this sort of thing happens in the evenings, right? But there I was, pulling in front of her ranch-style home an hour or two before sundown. It was a nice little place, lots of shrubs and flowers in boxes along the walk and bordering the wrap-around porch.

She met me on the porch. While her jeans and big t-shirt weren't awful, they didn't exactly say "fun" either. I was about to ask what she had in mind when she said, "Follow me," and led me around the house.

"I read this book once," she started. "The idea was people give and receive gestures of love different ways. Like to me, getting a gift is just something nice, but for you it might be how you say you care, you know? Gifts from others have real sentimental value, and when you give one, you take time to pick it out and it has real meaning behind it. You keep birthday cards and all that."

Her back yard was bigger than I expected, bordered by some trees and a creak. I followed her toward one of those metal sheds you can buy at a home repairs store. Where were we going, literally and figuratively? I said, "I barely look at greeting cards to be honest, but alright."

"One of them was 'acts of service'. Doing something for someone is important. Say your mom tells you she's sick, and you show up and cook dinner for her, because you want her to know you care." She slowed down outside the shed door. "I think that's you, it sounds a lot like how you care about simply satisfying and doing for a partner."

"That sounds like it could be true." Worth thinking about, but I didn't want to stand there being introspective. "Is that related to your back yard?"

Piper grabbed the shed's door and pulled it open with a horrid squeal, revealing a cluttered stack of boxes and tools. "That's why I'd like you to do something for me, and see if you like it." She pointed.

"You've got to be kidding."

"Nope." She padded inside and dragged the push mower out onto the grass. "Worth a try?"

I frowned and looked at the big yard. It definitely needed a trim. Hard work didn't scare me, but I'd barely met her. "You sure you're not exploiting me for some free yardwork?"

Piper crossed her arms over the mower's handle and shrugged. "I've known a sub who volunteered to clean this public play space, considered it not just charity but service. If that's not you, we can try something else. It was worth a shot...."

A memory bubbled up, bringing with it a laugh. "When I was ten I was watching one of those premium channels I shouldn't have been, and saw this movie where these cops chase are undercover on some BDSM vacation paradise. One slave says to the cop, 'Tell me how I may please you', and she says, 'Go paint my house.'"

She smiled. "Yeah, sorta like that."

With a sigh, I wagged my tail and said, "I'll try, but no painting."

"Deal."

"When you're done, come get me." She bent down, grabbing the pull-cord thing, and gave it a yank. "You know how to use one of these?"

"Sure," I bluffed, having only ever used a riding mower. How difficult could a pusher be? Push, grass gets cut. "Go on in, I've got this."

The second pull got the mower going. With a little wave, the raccoon turned and flounced back to the house, her tail waving.

It had a big handle to grab it and push, and two little levers attached to the handle, one above and one below. I squeezed the top lever and it revved up, grass spitting out the side. Guess that told it to run the blades.

Squeezing the top lever, I got to work. With a rider I typically went in a big square that got smaller and smaller, because turning a 180 was a big broad move that missed places. With the push I could swivel it around easily, so I went in a straight line, rotated, and mowed parallel to my first line. Systematic.

Alone with my thoughts, I mulled over what Piper had said. Dad always had enjoyed giving people thing she made, or do things for them, but I'd have chalked that up to him enjoying doing things with his hands and being cheap. Mom loved to cook for others, but she seemed to take far more happiness from compliments and gave them out in generous heaps. I guess that I did get some satisfaction out of helping and doing for someone else, outside of the bedroom.

Satisfied with the front, I killed the power and wheeled the mower back into the shed. I slid the back door open and poked my muzzle in. "Piper?"

After hollering back, she came into the kitchen. "How do you feel?"

"Hot and gross." Bits of yard dust and grass stuck to my fur, and I was panting from the work. Not wanting to track all of it inside, I stayed put on the patio for now.

Piper smiled, poured me a glass of cold water from the fridge and waited until after I'd lapped half of that down. "Okay, but how do you *feel*? Do you feel accomplished; is it like a gesture of affection?

A sigh. "Not really? Sorry. It is nice to have accomplished some hard work, but I'm wore out from pushing that thing so long."

"Oh well. You know it'll drive forward on its own if you squeezed the bottom lever, right?"

My ears laid back. "What? Oh come on."

She laughed. "Well, I have another idea, and this one a little more direct and likely to work, if you want to try that?"

In truth I wanted to go home, at least shoot for another day and at most give up. Instead I said, "Sure, but first I need to at least brush out my fur."

"How about a quick shower? Just enough to get damp? I have something I need to take care of, and for what I have in mind, it'll work if you do."

Now I was curious, but I agreed. Even with the glass of water working wonders, a cool shower would feel great.

Following her into the living room, I stopped dead.

Ten feet from me stood a robot frozen in mid-step.

Not a robot, I realized, but a really good cosplay. An open-faced motorcycle helmet had been painted chrome and given a mirrored visor over a rodent's muzzle, and the rat's tail had some kind of body sock made to look segmented and synthetic. The chrome body armor reflected the light like plastic, and wasn't far from those futuristic foot soldiers in that old space movie. Although those uniforms hadn't been crotchless.

If I hadn't been self-conscious before, I was now after getting a look at the rat's balls. .

Piper paused at the hall and turned. "Spades, I mentioned that others might be present sometimes. My housemate is big into objectification, being treated as less of a person, being made into an object, y'know. This is one of his...constructions."

Looking anywhere but the guy's balls, I said, "Okay."

Piper crossed over and snagged something on his back, twisting before pulling down with an audible *chunk*. The rat finished his step and strained.

He started to speak, something in a numb and lifeless tone, but the raccoon cut him off. "Go to your docking bay and power down."

Without missing a beat he strode away, the plastic pieces of his getup clacking together. When he passed, I got a look at his back—a solid backplate had a knob with numbers, something like a kitchen timer but larger, and beside that a big lever with a ball at the end, like joystick from an arcade cabinet, angled downwards.

Piper waved me on, and we continued to the spacious master bathroom. She turned to me. "I'm sorry. Zack and I haven't had schedules that meshed well lately, and he gets *really* into character. Usually it's low key with him, all I have to do is play along, and before you were done I'd sent him to his room to end the session, but I forgot about the timer pack."

"Timer pack?" I hoped she didn't hear the dubiousness in my voice.

"The thing on his back, he built it like a giant windup toy. When the timer goes off, it clicks and he'll stop moving."

"That's uh," I groped for something inoffensive, "not practical for a robot."

She rolled her eyes but smiled. "Practicality isn't the point. It's an element of control, almost like time-based bondage, except purely mental." Waving her hands as if to dismiss the tangent, Piper said, "I didn't want you to see him in-character and think I was neglecting you, or anything."

"No, it's fine." I tried not to think about his weighty balls. "What're you wanting me to do?"

She looked me in the eye, hesitating only a moment. "I want you to bathe me."

My ears flicked back. "I... really?"

"Yes. Call it 'worship'. I want you to pamper me, *attend* to me, like a servant." Tilting her head and looking up at me through her hair, Piper grinned. Even without the proper equipment I felt it, right in my gut. "How does that sound??"

Why was my mouth suddenly dry? "Uh good, good."

"Good. I'll show you what I want when you're done. Now get in there."

The shower didn't take long. Standing in front of the cool spray long enough to feel good left me a bit wetter than I was wanting, but oh well. If I waited any longer, thoughts of what was about to happen might have filtered in, but I focused on the water soaking into my fur. A vigorous shake and brushing in the tub later took care of the mess, and I let my fur air-dry.

A knock bounced off the door. "All done? You decent?"

"Don't think I'll ever be decent, but one sec." I stepped out on the fuzzy mat and pulled on my underwear—being seen naked was something I didn't want. Probably not something to come up much in the future. "Okay."

"Get the bathwater going, nice and toasty."

Toasty water spilled over my paw and into the plugged tub. My stomach was full of butterflies again, which took to flying about when she called me out of the bathroom.

Why was I so nervous?

"Next time I'll expect you to get my clothes ready, but I've set them out on the bed. Take those inside, and find some towels. Set those up." I went about in a rush, gathering them and laying them out on the commode.

In she came. After a glance around the room she raised her arms, swished her tail, and said, "Undress me."

I swallowed. Hooking fingers under her shirt, I peeled it up and over her outstretched arms, then folded it before setting it aside. This earned me her tail brushing across my stomach. The bra next, though I went a little slower, rubbing my thumbs through the fur on her back.

"Mmm." Her smile was almost audible.

Bra left on the pile, I went for her pants and worked them down. Had her panties been something racy, I think it would have hurt me, the idea that I was missing out. There was still a little pang of...maybe loss, as I marveled at her fine behind gripped in the maroon boyshorts, knowing I'd never be buried in a lovely woman like this again. For that reason the panties went fast.

Thankfully she didn't turn and let me gawk, make a show for me. Instead she stepped into the tub and sank. "Ahh." She leaned back, briefly soaking her hair.

I'd started to feel awkward at not knowing what to do with myself, like I was interrupting her, when she turned a luxurious smile up at me. "Now, shampoo me."

"What?"

Amusement warmed her face, but her tone was casually firm. "Boy, kneel." She aimed her finger at me, then down at the fuzzy mat.

"Yes ma'am." My knees sunk into the damp fuzz.

Aiming her digit at a bottle, she said, "Shampoo." Finally that digit turned to her hair. "Me."

Dumbly I snatched it up and squeezed a glob into my palm, then began to soap her tresses. The raccoon's sigh was comfortable, and as I worked, I rubbed fingers into the back of her head, her scalp and temples, her neck. She cooed at me, and I could've kept going, but she was quite lathered. Letting my fingers rinse in the tub, I said, "Done."

She dunked and rose, then lifted to her knees. "Now, my back."

It went like that, rubbing chemicals into each piece of her. While being brief with her breasts, my hands were slow on her legs, her eyes on mine as I traced calves and thighs. I caught her breath rising just a hint, and she "mmmm'd" for me, showing a smile she knew exactly what she was doing. The bath trailed on forever, and when it was done I was left breathless and ready to go again.

Piper rose out of the water. Her standing there, soaked to the bone, cleared some of the spell I'd been under. The fur hung off of her like drenched carpet, and I could see spots longer than the surrounding areas, places that needed trimming. I wrapped her in the towel and helped her over the tub.

Towel first, then dryer, and soon that brown pelt was fluffy. "Comb's there." Thing slowed down again as I slid the bristles through her fur, turning fluff into silky, straight strands. Once more I had the opportunity to touch every region, slow and precise this time. She was still and silent until I brought out a larger brush and went to her tail, then her hair, both spots earning sighs, her body leaning back against mine.

I'd always loved women's hair, but had never groomed it. With it flowing over my fingers as I stroked through it, the wave of it beneath the passes of the brush, I was flat-out wagging even if wolves weren't supposed to wag.

When finished, I dressed her. Odd putting clothes *on* a woman for a change. It lacked the echo of sexuality undressing her had.

She turned to me, resting a palm on my chest. "How do you feel?"

I exhaled. "Relaxed and excited and satisfied...just warm all over." I could get used to this. "The same kind of submissive buttons are getting pushed."

"Good." Her eyes shone like precious stones in the sun. "That was luxurious by the way." Pulling away, she turned and sashayed from the bathroom.

Our sessions expanded from there. Soon I was learning how to give massages, trim and paint her claws, apply her makeup. Instead of feeling like I was seen as some kind of girlfriend—to braid our hair and chat about boys—I took pride in giving her the kind of attention she deserved, making her feel adored, leaving her looking good. She once used the word "worship", and yeah it fit.

Maybe six or seven months of this and things went sideways.

Piper met me at the door in a corset, boots and skimpy panties, all a dark purple. While it looked delicious on her, sexy dress-up was not part of our thing. I hesitated. "Are you with someone else?" It was a night set aside for me, and an envious pang ricocheted through my skull.

"No. Well, not exactly." Forcing a smile, she snagged my shirt and pulled. "Get in here." When the door closed, she turned to me and took a deep breath. "I want to try something. Not sure if you'll like it though, and it wouldn't be right to push you in without any warning."

"That doesn't sound ominous at all." The poker face I offered was strained.

"I want to make a point to you, and share something important. But to do that," she hesitated a moment, then pushed forward, "you have to watch me have sex."

No. "I...don't know." I fought to not tuck my tail. Refusal was buzzing under my fur; it was what my gut said, but was that the right thing? Seeing her that first time had been just as viscerally scary, but I'd taken the chance. Maybe it was different now, how long we'd been together, the way things had changed, maybe I could push through whatever pain I was having. Ripping a band-aid off.

If there was anyone I trusted to try this with, it would be her.

"Are you sure?" The raccoon reached out and squeezed my arm. "I don't want to hurt you.'"

"Hell no I'm not sure, but I think I can try."

The prelude to a smile nudged at the corner of her

muzzle. "Well that's a good start. We'll use safewords, the typical red yellow green, okay?"

Stomach in knots, I nodded, and she led me into the bedroom. A comfy chair had been set beside the head of the bed. "Sit and close your eyes," she directed, and stroked my shoulders and face nice and slow. It didn't take long under her fingers for me to relax, at least a semblance of it.

Piper's fingers withdrew. "Give me just a minute."

This would be fine. Piper knew what she was doing, and we were close. We—the sound of plastic clacking interrupted my thoughts, and I looked to the source.

Piper was already in, and following her was her roommate in his robot getup. She held a clunky kind of remote as big as a paperback novel. She climbed up the bed, rolled over on her back, and pressed one of the buttons on the remote, lighting up a blue LED with an audible chirp. "Come here, remove my panties, and engage cunnilingus."

The rat climbed up the bed and reached for her hips.

We were really doing this, weren't we?

Piper turned her head to me. "Spades." The concern in her voice lifted my ears. "Spades you're breathing hard." I was? "Look at me. Look into my eyes."

Hers were hazel, big and most importantly right now, intense. She stared hard into me, both commanding and compassionate. "Keep looking at me, because I'm just looking at you." Even when her breath caught, and she squirmed, she kept staring at me.

I didn't look below her chin. Even so, I couldn't help picturing her roommate in that goofy-ass outfit with his nose in her crotch. It was hard not to look away, especially when her eyes half-lidded and her breath picking up, when I knew she was enjoying herself.

Enjoying herself with someone who wasn't me, because I couldn't do this. Well, I could go down on her, yes, but—

The remote chirped again. "Extend erection."

I held back a laugh, the dirty look she shot me helping me swallow it.

"Spades, what color is it?"

I blinked. "Color?"

"The stoplight, what color is it?"

Breathe in, breathe out. "Green."

"Good. Here we go." The raccoon rolled over, lifting her hips, and the remote chirped. "Insert erection, engage sexual protocol."

I could hear the rat moving, sense the activity, but Piper kept her eyes on me. The moment he entered her was obvious, her ears flicking and her lips tightening, which slid a knife in me.

"What point are you trying to make here?" Was my voice shaking a little?

"Give me your hand." She held hers over the bed's edge. I took it, and she squeezed tight. Girl had a good grip. "I'm being pleasured by a toy. It's not important to me, it's a tool, nothing more. What's important to me is you, you're here with me, as I please myself. Do you understand?"

"Yeah." Even I wasn't too convinced by that. Calling him an unimportant tool must've fit into his objectification fetish, so that made some kind of sense. He was still another person, still a guy who was doing what I couldn't, was a guy with—no, I needed to think of it like she was saying, because my tail was tucked between the chair's legs.

"It's...yellow."

She nodded, used the remote. "Slower." The hand

holding mine squeezed again, and she stroked her thumb through the fur. "I care about you, Spades, and I want to share this with you. Even if you're not actively participating, it's still meaningful you're here, involved with this."

Yet I wanted to be the one fucking her. Missed the feel of pussy, of orgasming. Our sessions had let me not think about it, but here, now, I couldn't not picture her writhing under me. The sound of their bodies moving, the smell of them drove claws into my back.

At that moment her roommate thrust hard, and I could hear his balls slapping her thigh.

I stood up and made for the door. "Red," I said as an afterthought.

"Stop. I need you to stop! Red, dammit," she growled at Zack. "Spades!"

"Wait." Piper caught my arm as I made it to the living room. I definitely did no tneed to see her mid-fuck, her crotch wet, her hair mussed, her breath fast. "I'm sorry if that made you uncomfortable, I didn't mean to bust your balls, I—""

The look on my face must have been bad, because she took a step back. "Oh Spades I am so sorry, I didn't mean it like that."

"No, it's fine. I get it." I waved a hand, finding somewhere to not look at her. "You didn't mean it that way. I get what you were trying to do here." Kind of. "Not mad at you, but I need fresh air, I need to go."

That's how I left her, tail between my legs.

The phone rang, a surprise given how late it was. I was playing poker online because the usual game got cancelled. Seeing the name set my ears back and brought a dark mood. Even after a week I hadn't yet swallowed my feelings enough to talk. Already I'd folded and clicked the 'set out next round' but hesitated over the phone. After waffled until halfway through the last ring, I answered.

"James? Hi, I...Are you busy right now?" Piper's voice shook. Bad connection, or was she walking somewhere?

"Not really, but it's—-"

"Because I really need to talk to someone right now." No mistaking the thick warble of held-back tears in her voice.

I sat up straight, my ears alert. "Are you hurt, stranded somewhere? Everything okay?"

She laughed poorly, the sound too tightly wound and about to snap. "I'm safe, but I've had a shock and, and I want to be held. Listen to me, I sound like a wimp. And I know I fucked up last time—-"

"Sure, anything, yes. Are you okay to drive or should I come to you?"

Another of those broken laughs. "Your place, I need to get out of here, I think." I gave her the address and straightened up a few things.

The first thing she did when I opened the door was hug me. A solid squeeze that she clearly did not want to let go of. "Can I have something to drink?"

I pulled back. "Sure, I have ice tea, juic—"

"A drink drink. I don't care as long as it's hard."

While I hadn't known Piper long enough to guess if she was the histrionic type or not, I knew this wasn't your typical drama by her outfit: a pair of pajama pants and a nice blouse with the done-up buttons off by one. For that reason alone the glass got more vodka than orange juice.

"Thanks." She took it, sipped, and her whiskers flared in a cringe. It didn't stop the second pull.

Sitting next to her, I tentatively put an arm around her, and she pressed right in. This close to her, I couldn't help but sniff and picked up the lingering trace of a different female, something probably canine but it was hard to tell.

Before even starting she sighed, a shake once more in her voice.

"You going to tell me what's up, or kill me with worry?"

Piper laughed weakly. "You look pretty fine."

"Good pokerface. Come on, you're safe here."

Another sigh, another sip. "I messed up royally tonight and endangered a sub. Kate is the sweetest girl you can imagine, even moreso when she subs, and I had her trussed up and she started acting like a brat. At first I rolled with it, but her comments got meaner, and she started growling at me, baring her teeth--anyone else I'd have thought they were trying to dom from the bottom, or maybe trying to play a game, but not Kate. It felt really wrong."

All of that came out in a rush, but when she stopped, Piper held the quiet. Instead of prompting her, I leaned over and nuzzled between her ears, squeezing her shoulders. She shook just a little.

"When I asked if she was okay, she said 'I'll never tell you'. She even tried to bite me when I went to untie her wrists." Piper pressed her palm into her face. "I forgot about her diabetes. When blood sugar's too low, they can go a little crazy; she'd been so excited earlier today that eating slipped her mind. When I got some juice and cookies down her, she said she thought I was interrogating her, going to torture her and put her under the back ."

She looked up at me then. Piper wasn't crying, or

trying to hold it back, but I could hear the ache in her voice. "She was in trouble, and I missed it. I was too busy playing around, and I *missed it*." Waving her hands around to emphasize sent the drink sloshing, and she seemed to notice it for the first time since that second sip.

I took it from her and set it aside. When I turned back she leaned into my arms and I held her.

"How can she trust me again? How can I trust me again?" Piper said into my neck. "First I mess up with you, now this...."

She went quiet, and I stroked her back a few moments before I realized she was waiting for me. "Do you need me to listen silently, reassure you that you're wrong and everything's okay, or tell you what I think?"

The sad smile was clear in her voice. "If I said the second one, I'd be pretty delusional, huh?"

I sat back, enough to nuzzle her forehead. "Nothing wrong with spilling without looking for advice. You only want to be heard. Now may not be the best time even if you did want an outside opinion."

She shook her head, ears folding back. "No, this is serious and I can't hide from it with warm fuzzies. Give me the lecture."

Points for her. "What happened with Kate, afterwards?"

"Once we had her blood sugar resembling normal, she was fine. Drove herself home."

"Sure, but what did she do? Did she blame you? Yell at you?"

Piper shook her head, the motion rustling on my shoulder. "Apologized over and over, told me I didn't do anything wrong. Typical Kate. Asked if we could reschedule."

"Sounds to me like she still trusts you."

The raccoon sat back and gave me a stare. "Of course she'd say th—"

"No she wouldn't, not if she was upset with you. She wasn't hurt, you picked up on something being wrong, you acted and she's okay."

"But it took me so long to see it." She looked down, finally noticed her buttons were askew, and began fixing them. "I was reckless."

Catching her muzzle, I tilted her face to me so I could bump my nose against hers. "What matters is you caught it before it was too late. The only thing you can do in the future is ask the sub for status updates more often, take a step back and assess them regularly. You're not a mind reader, what else should you be doing?"

"Be perfect," Piper said, in a pouty and insincere tone, the corners of her muzzle wavering into a weak smile. "I don't know. But thanks."

That was good enough. From her. At least I gave her something to think about. Hugging her shoulder again, I cuddled down in her. She relaxed. At least I could reassure her.

I could. The thought froze me.

She came to me. Not any of her kinkster friends, not another friend period, hell she didn't even call Dr. Shapiro.

I asked, "Would you like to stay the night?"

Against my shoulder she said, "I didn't really bring anything to wear..."

"Well technically you brought at least half of something." Looking down, she realized she was in pajama pants and sighed. Chuckling, I added, "It's not like I haven't seen you naked. Would you like to sleep with me?"

Piper tilted her muzzle.

"I can set up the couch, but I'm willing to bet it's been a while since you nodded off in someone's arms."

"Alright," she said. The zing in my chest surprised me, told me that offer was important and I wasn't aware of it. I went about doing the nightly preparations, and for the first time in a long time, I was comfortable with myself.

BUZZED
JONATHAN W. THURSTON

I still can't believe I'm doing this, Zack thought to himself as he walked down Hazel Avenue, his hooves clacking against the pavement noisily. He and Spencer had been dating for six months, and they had decided to hold off on having sex...until now. Over dinner one night the previous week, Spencer had confided to Zack that he was "not very traditional" when it came to sex. Zack, even as traditional as he was in his own sexual behaviors, had smiled and asked to know more. After all, he loved Spencer and wanted to do whatever he could to make his partner happy.

He smiled to himself. *He's probably just some 50 Sheens of Grey kind of guy. Likes tying boys up or using toys, or maybe likes taking pics while he does it.* Zack shrugged and kicked a stone as he walked. *Not too big a deal. It's still just sex...just with a different flavor. Hell, I wouldn't judge him even if he liked wearing one of those human-suits, as weird-looking and perverted as those are.*

And now, as he walked from work to Spencer's job, a car repair shop, he was expecting a night of what Spencer promised to be some "kinky fun." Zack shook his head, getting some of the hair from his mane out of his eyes. *I don't know how fun it will be, but I'm in this to win it...and I want to show him that I won't be that boring gay guy. I'll show him.*

Pulling out his cell phone, he checked to see if the raccoon had messaged him since he left work. There was just one short text: "u ready?" A small shiver crept up Zack's spine, but he shook it off, typing quickly in response, "Absolutely. Hope you are ;)". He didn't feel as confident as he was trying to come off, and that was alright. Hopefully, whatever it was that Spencer was into wouldn't require too much dominance or confidence on Zack's part.

He thrust the phone back into the front pocket of his hoodie and hunched his shoulders, fighting back the autumn breeze. Spencer had told him not to bother wearing much, and Zack had done as instructed: some shorts that cut off six inches above the knee and a red zipper hoodie that barely kept him warm.

He could remember the conversation they had after that dinner the previous week.

"Are you sure, Zack? We can discuss limits and boundaries if you want. I don't want you to be too scared or anything," Spencer had said.

"No...I don't care what it is. I trust you. I am game for whatever. Just don't take me out into the woods and kill me," Zack had said, hoping Spencer couldn't feel his heat rising.

"Still...you don't want any safe words or anything like that?" Spencer had said this with concern in his voice: it was true, but he also had a sly grin on his face, and that grin had given Zack pause.

"Y-yes, I'm sure. I'll be fine, Spence. And I'll show you next week. Just name the day, and I'll be ready."

"Alright," Spencer had replied, rubbing a paw across Zack's bare leg under the restaurant table, brushing once against his crotch, already hard from the intrigue alone.

As he thought back on the conversation, Zack started to get worried. He kept trying to think of what the worst thing Spencer could be into. If there were multiple guys waiting for him at the shop, it would give Zack reason to blush, but it would be fine. If Spencer brought huge-knotted dildos, it might be rough, but Zack would manage, even if sore the next day. If Spencer was into outdoors and wanted to tie Zack up to a tree, the most Zack would have to worry about would be getting poison ivy or bug bites. He just couldn't envision what would have warranted Spencer's knowing and sly grin.

His tail swished once when he saw the blue neon sign in the distance: "Coon's Car Repairs." Spencer was the only raccoon in the shitty town that was Hazel Hollow, so all his customers simply knew him as Coon. And that was just part of his local charm: this quirky, grease-furred, snarky, doesn't-give-a-damn-what-anyone-thinks raccoon. That attitude was just one of the reasons Zack had come to love him.

His heartbeat accelerated as he began to see more of the building through the trees. The main office was dark with a barely visible CLOSED sign in the window; yet, there was one of the three garages with all its lights still on, a silver minivan straight from the 90s resting in the center of the lights as if it were some brand new car model, loud and proud. Zack snickered. *It probably belongs to some eighty-year-old couple, and it's probably sat in their own garage for the past decade, collecting dust. I'm sure Spence was pissed to get that piece of junk in.*

He made it to the front of the garage and peered in, standing in the entrance. Surprisingly, there weren't any other cars in the shop--maybe the others were out back--and the place seemed decently clean, almost abandoned. There was only the minivan, its headlights almost staring at Zack, questioning his very presence.

"Um...Spencer?" Zack said to the empty air around him. He cleared his throat and tried again, louder, "Spencer, are you here?" *Maybe he doesn't know it's me and thinks I'm a customer or something.* "Uh, Spence? It's me, Zack. Where are you?"

"Heeeeey, babe," Spencer called, his speech slurring. Zack froze at the entrance to the garage, his eyes wide. As Spencer ambled toward him, his steps forced and blundering, Zack realized he was drunk. Zack hadn't seen Spencer this drunk since that one time he had a fight with his parents and made Zack come to pick him up. They had went to a decrepit church that had been shut down years ago, and Spencer had thrown bricks through the windows, yelling obscenities that had to have woken people that night.

"Why are you drunk, Spence?" Zack's ears were flat, and his tail tucked between his legs like a canine, but he still stood his ground.

Spencer lurched forward, and Zack saw the same grin he had seen a week ago. "Becaaaause, babe. This fucking old couple came in this morning and dropped that clunker off. Do you...do you wanna know what's wrong with it?"

Zack stared back and said softly, "What?"

Spencer spread his arms wide and laughed. "*Everything!* The radiator's sssshot, the brakes were cut, the tires need replacing, the engine needs replacing, even the goddamn A/C's fucked. And you wanna know what topped it all off? The icing on top of the...the cake?"

Zack shook his head. He knew Spencer was pissed, and that scared him a bit. Spencer had never been angry at Zack, but Zack knew Spencer was one of those cursing drunks who'd curse out anyone and anything, with a touch of vandalism thrown in. Still, he felt a surge of relief. Maybe that meant they wouldn't do anything tonight after all.

"The fuckers tried to haggle the price with me. This ain't the nineteen-fucking-sixties. I do everything by computer nowadays anyway. Cheapskates." He belched and stepped forward again, putting a dark-striped paw on Zack's shoulder. "But I don't give a shit. You're here now, and we're gonna have the night of our lives, right?"

Zack managed a smile and felt his tail twitch in interest despite his nerves. "Absolutely."

"Sssso," Spencer mumbled, his breath almost toxic to Zack's flaring nostrils. "Are you sure you want to do this? Once we ssssstart, there's no...there's no going back, a'ight?"

"Of course, I'm sure," Zack replied with his best attempt at a sly wink. "I told you my grandpa's a fox. I'll prove it to you tonight. Just wait and see."

"Heh," Spencer laughed. "That's my boy." He hovered there for a moment, breathing shallow breaths as his eyes struggled to fix on Zack. "A'ight, I need to go out back and uh...grab some...*equipment* for us. I want you to stay here and strip for me, 'kay? Just throw your clothes wherever."

Zack looked over his shoulder back to the street, and he was tempted to ask if he was sure no one would come by, seeing the garage light on. But he turned back to the raccoon and nodded, "Sounds good."

"Good." Spencer leaned in and planted a kiss on Zack's mouth, his whiskers tickling the small pony's nose, before half-walking half-lurching to the back office.

Zack let out a sigh of relief. *This will be fine. He's not that pissed. And he's being sweet. This might actually be fun.* He unzipped his hoodie and carefully folded it against one of the concrete pillars at the edge of the garage. Then, refusing to look back at the road for any reason, he unbuttoned his shorts and slid them off his legs, too. His auburn fur stood on end immediately, the chill of the night air penetrating his skin. He wrapped his thin arms around his chest and looked around the garage, trying to find something to distract him from constantly checking to see if someone was coming. His ears flicked when he heard a rattling sound.

I knew it, Zack thought as Spencer came out from the back with a few chain lengths of various sizes. "Where do you want me?"

Spencer grinned. "You're ssssupposed to say, 'Where do you want me, sssssir.'"

Zack felt heat rise in his face, and his ears flattened. "Where do you want me, sir?"

He motioned with his pointed snout to the hood of the old minivan with the cracked silver paint. "Get on the car...on your back...booooy." Spencer said the word "boy" with a deep and commanding drawl.

Zack swallowed as he approached it. Easing back

on his paws, he climbed on top of the hood and laid down, his head almost touching the windshield and his hindpaws dangling over the front bumper. Spencer went to work immediately, starting by spreading Zack's arms out and chaining his wrists to the side mirrors. Next, he bound Zack's legs to the front bumper, just as spread out, so his hooves pressed uncomfortably against the headlights.

When Spencer was done, he went around to the side of the car and picked something up from within the car. Zack could hear the muffled sounds of shuffling around in the seats. The windows must have been open. "Alriiiight," Spencer called as he walked back over to stand beside Zack's right wrist. "How does that feel, boy? Nice and tight?"

Zack nodded. "Yes--"

Spencer shoved a rag into Zack's mouth. It was a filthy grease rag from the day's work, and the acrid taste almost brought tears to the horse's eyes on contact. Spencer held out a small piece of bungee cord and wrapped it around Zack's head so he could not spit the rag out. "Good boy. Now, I'll be back in a bit. Hang tight." And without another word or glance, Spencer ran off behind the car. Zack could hear the raccoon's footfalls fade away behind the garage.

Zack started counting in his head, trying not to focus on the taste in his mouth. *One...two...three...four...See, Zack? The taste's not so bad if you don't think about it.* He looked down at his body chained to the hood of this car, and he wondered what the couple who owned it would think if they knew two gay guys had fucked on it the night before. The idea made his cock twitch against his stomach, its tip starting to flare. A minute passed. Another passed in the same silence.

Tilting his head around to try to see the raccoon, his eyes suddenly widened; he heard a car approaching from behind. Even as his heart pounded, worrying who was going to see him tied spread-eagle to the front of some old couple's car, the car pulled up beside him, a red Honda Civic, with Spencer in the driver's seat. Zack sighed through his nose. *What is he doing? If he's taking me somewhere in that car, why did he go through the trouble of tying me up in the first place?*

Spencer stepped out of the driver's seat, not turning the car off, holding several thick cables and a much smaller cord with a dark metal bulb at the end. Zack raised a brow in perplexity, but his cock betrayed his curiosity.

Spencer chuckled. "Oh, is my pony boy ex...excited?" He hiccupped as he walked around to the front of the Civic. "Be patient. Just a little bit loooonger." He popped open the hood of the car and started attaching the cables. Zack squinted.

Those are just jumper cables. What is he doing? Does he just get off on fixing cars while there's a naked guy in the shop with him?

Then, the raccoon, his face alight with that mischievous grin, connected the thick jumper cables with the thinner cable with the bulb. Recognition hit Zack like a hundred volts. The bulb was a butt plug. Spencer had rigged a car battery to serve as some kind of electronic-stimulation butt plug. Zack started struggling against the chains, but he did not cry out, unwilling to completely give up now.

Spencer walked up to the horse on the hood of the minivan, holding the plug carefully in one gloved paw as if it were a bottle he was about to give to a baby. "Aw, c'mon, you're not quitting yet, are you?"

31

Zack found himself wondering what Spencer would do if he *really* tried to put up a struggle, if the raccoon would call it quits...or do it anyway.

Spencer smirked. "Don't worry. This isn't any stronger than any other e-stim device. Promise." To prove his point, he removed a glove from one paw and tapped the tip of the plug a few times. "A little shock, but it's not that bad."

Calming his anxieties the best he could, Zack stopped squirming and closed his eyes. *Maybe this won't be that bad. It can't be that bad...right? It should feel like--*

While he had closed his eyes, Spencer had stepped forward the rest of the way and slammed the plug under his tail, pushing it into Zack's tailhole in one swift movement.

Even as the car started shooting small jolts of electricity through his anus, his cock hardened to full erection. His mind was regretting this whole night, but he was powerless to do anything about it now, and his body was relenting to a mixture of pain and pleasure he had never dared to imagine. He pushed against the chain in all directions, trying to make the plug somehow comfortable, but it kept teasing against his prostate, sending pulses through his balls.

Once he started moaning against the grease rag, Spencer climbed on top of the car, too, straddling Zack's hips, the raccoon's rump teasing along Spencer's cock. Spencer reached forward and undid the cable around Zack's snout, removing the rag in turn. The horse moaned loud and shuddered under Spencer's weight. "F-f-f-*fuck*, Spence. I'm g-g-gonna cum soon!"

Spencer pulled his pants off, leaving them in a crumpled pile on the stone floor, and moved quickly. Crawling up Zack's body, he knelt in front of the horse's face and pressed his cock to the long snout. "Open up, pony *bitch*," Spencer snarled. "You'll cum when I do."

Zack closed his eyes and tried to concentrate on *not* cumming as the raccoon mounted his face like a dog and began humping. The pressure in his groin was intense. Each pulse from the plug sent him closer and closer to the edge. It felt like needles skating across his skin, but, at the same time, it felt like he was being jacked off from the *inside,* and that feeling was incredible.

Grabbing the pony's ears, Spencer started thrusting harder, his cock sliding over Zack's tongue and barely pressing against his throat. "Fuck, boy, c'mon. You ready for my cum in your throat?"

Zack could only moan in response as the very dirty talk pushed him over the edge.

"*Fuck!*" Spencer roared, his head tilting backward. The raccoon's seed filled Zack's muzzle and throat in a gushing flood, the salt in the mess seeming to spark and flare against his tongue like sugarless Pop Rocks. Zack's eyes opened wide, but all he could see was the white fur below Spencer's stomach, the smell of grease and sweat filling and tickling his nostrils. Zack's cock shot in time with the buzzing pulses of the car battery, three huge bursts of cum spraying onto the pony's chest and throat before dribbling out in a pool at his navel. His insides seemed to throb, swollen around the plug, eager to get it out now.

Sliding off Zack and the car, Spencer replaced the grease rag in Zack's mouth, but now, even Zack was too exhausted to care, much less protest. Spencer swayed over to the driver's side of the Civic beside them and collapsed in the seat, laying his head back against the headrest. "Ffffuck, Zack. You're better than I...than I thought you'd be."

Zack grinned inwardly and sighed in contention, closing his eyes. *I'm glad,* he thought. *Now I'd appreciate it if you got this plug out of me. I swear, I'm gonna be sore as hell tomorrow.* The thought made him even happier, though. He had pleased Spencer, had enjoyed himself, and had definitely survived the night. But now he was ready to clean up--he hated being covered in fluids like this, from both cars and naked bodies--and get some sleep.

Zack looked over at his mate and exhaled deeply, ready to embrace him and go home...but the raccoon wasn't moving. *Spence? Spence?* Zack thought, his heart racing from the sudden lack of attention. He stared hard at Spencer, and then he noticed the raccoon's slack jaw, his left forepaw dangling beside the seat...and he heard Spencer let out a snore.

Zack's breathing relaxed, but his cock began to harden again, unable to stop or abate the pulsing sensation in his ass. *Dammit,* he thought. *He can't leave me like this all night. I'll be...* He whined against the gag. *I'll be cumming all night like this...and what if someone finds me in the morning before he gets up?* He whined louder, but Spencer's snores stayed louder. Stretching his legs against the chain, he tried again to find a more comfortable position with the limited range of movement the chains offered, but he was stuck.

His only hope was that Spencer would wake up soon... or that the battery would die before the old couple came back to pick up their car.

ALL WORK AND NO PLAY
TJ MINDE

The giant otter pulled his pants over his jock and tucked his shirt in. "Okay Lucas, I think I'm almost ready to go." Art finished buttoning up his polo before looking to his lover.

"You sure you want to do this, babe?" the smaller otter asked from the bed

Art walked to the side of the bed and kissed the Lucas' forehead. "Yeah. I want you to enjoy your day off. And this sounds like fun for the both of us." He winked.

"But didn't Dennis say you were in line for a promotion here soon?" Lucas asked.

The taller otter nodded. "He did. But with the client coming in soon, the call center manager is running around like a chicken with his head cut off." He smoothed the last of the wrinkles out of his shirt. "He'll be so busy, things will probably be a bit more lax until they're here."

Lucas nodded. "Okay. You've been there longer than I have. I think I'mma lay here a bit more before I get my day going."

"Sounds like a plan." Art grabbed his wallet and keys and droped them into his pocket. "Well, I'm heading out." He kissed the other otter on the muzzle. "Have fun, love." With another wink, Art walked out the door.

Art tapped out a beat on the steering wheel. "Traffic sucks," he sung to himself. With a final flourish, the otter flopped back against the seat and let the car roll forward. Pressing a brown paw between his legs, Art sighed while attempting to adjust himself. *Today's going to be interesting,* he thought with a smile.

Resting his head on his balled fist, Art turned on the radio and flipped from station to station. Before he could decide on one, he felt a paw pads rub against his shaft. Art closed his eyes and grinned. *We're starting already, huh?*

He spread his legs out of habit as he reached for his cell in his pocket. With claws around the case, he opened his eyes; red brake lights stopped feet ahead of him. "Shit." His phone clattered to the floor as he grabbed the wheel and hit the brakes. The seat belt locked against his chest before slamming the otter back against the seat.

Art let out a shudder, both at the paw between his legs and the near accident. With his foot firmly on the break, he felt around for his phone. Once he had it, he texted one word to Lucas:

Driving

A moment later, the pads stopped teasing him. Art sighed again and grabbed at his bulge harder. "So that's how today's gonna be? The day will probably go quicker at least."

As the otter walked up to his cubicle, a snow leopard about his height stood waiting for him. "Hey dude, where you been?"

"Come on, Dennis. Did you not even bother to look at my schedule, Mr. Team Lead?"

The snow leopard rolled his eyes. "Please. Who has time for that?"

"Well, you have time to stand by my computer while I'm on break."

"Psh, details." Dennis waved his paw in dismissal. "Is your significant otter doing anything special on his day off?"

Art coughed and looked over his shoulder at his team lead. "Are you serious?" he grinned. "Does that make me the *insignificant* otter?" Dennis smiled like a snow leopard that caught a canary as he crossed his arms over his chest. "You're lucky you're a friend, or we might be in HR." The otter shook his head and ran his paw over his muzzle. "He's probably hanging out around the house, I'd assume."

The snow leopard nodded. "Good. He needs a day to relax. Sorry I couldn't approve your PTO, too."

"Not the end of the world." Art typed in his password, unlocking his screen. "At least one of us has a three-day weekend."

"Speaking of Lucas, he and I were talking last week." Dennis' voice got lower.

"Oh?"

With a toothy grin, the snow leopard leaned in closer. "Yeah. Did he tell you about this thing I found online?" Art raised an eyebrow. "It started off as shipping tech, but didn't quite work on that scale. But it worked great as a sex toy."

Art tried to sound earnest. "You don't say?" He spun his chair around, facing Dennis.

"Yeah, it looks like a jock strap, but on the inside is a portal. Slip your dick in and it comes out through the paired receiver. Lucas mentioned you two wanted to try something kinky, but wasn't sure what. I thought this could be a simple start."

The otter's dick twitched at the thought. "Heh. Could be interesting." He fought to keep his paws above his waist. "Sounds like a toy meant to tease."

"Oh, *does it*. I mean, you can't do much to help yourself along in the scene or anything. You're at the mercy of the dom." Dennis' tail lashed about in excitement as he spoke.

"I'll definitely have to talk to Lucas about that then. Sounds like fun." He looked at his watch. "Well, back to calls. Fifteen minutes just flies by."

Dennis rolled his eyes. "Try not to have *too* much fun." He clapped the otter on the shoulder and walked away.

"*Fun?*" Art watched as the snow leopard pulled out his cell phone. The otter shrugged. *He's just being a smart ass.* With a dismissive shake of the head he groped between his legs again. *There's no way Dennis knows.*

The otter put on his headset and, a moment later, a beep chimed in his ear. "Thank you for calling. My name's Art. How can we help you today?"

"I want to know why my bill is so darn high this month," a woman said.

The otter's claws danced across the keys.. "We can help you with that. And who am I speaking with?"

"Susan Collins, young man. But please call me Suzi."

Art nodded out of habit. "Of course, Suzi. Let me verify your account, and then I can review your bill with you." Once he had access, the otter opened an image of the document, skimmed it, and rubbed his paws together. "Okay, Mrs. Collins, thank you for your patience."

"Oh, honey, 'Suzi,' *please*," his customer said. "Mrs. Collins was my mother."

"Yes, Suzi. I'm sorry." The otter closed his eyes, shaking his head. "So I've looked over your bill and I found the problem; last month you went over your allotted minutes by quite a bit."

"I did? Oh, fiddlesticks. My sister went into the hospital and I was so worried about her, pup."

I'm not that *young. At least it's a simple call.*

Out of habit, Art nodded. "Of course. I certainly understand that worry; my mother was in the hospital last year and I called her every day."

"You're such a good boy."

"I try. But back to your bill, ma'am: the overages on your plan are what made it higher this month."

"Is there anything we can do about those charges?" Suzi asked.

The otter nodded his head again. "Oh, of course."

Before he could continue, a finger ran along his shaft again.

Art caught his breath between his teeth.

"You okay, pup?"

"Yeah, sorry. I injured my knee years ago and weather affects it," he lied as he pressed a paw between his legs. "I'll be fine."

The fingers change to a full grip, sliding along his length.

"Excuse me." The otter hit mute and let out a soft squeak with a smile. *Take two while on a call?* Art huffed out a breath as he looked at a digital picture on his desk and Lucas looked back smiling that sly grin. *You wicked little thing. But I can make it.* He took another breath before returning to the call. "As I was saying, there are a few options available." He smiled. "We can make some changes to your plan that will not only help you with those overages, but can get you more minutes as well."

"Really?"

"Of course." Art felt a soft breath against his swelling shaft. "T-there are two routes we could take." He set a paw over his eyes. "The first option available is more minutes in general." He rattled off three different plans as he looked at his notes, comparing cost and savings.

"Those don't sound too bad," Suzi said. "But are there any other options."

"We always have o-options." As Art reached the last word, the sensation changed to moist lips running the length of his cock. The otter hit the mute button and let out another squeak, wiggling from side to side in his chair. "Oh boy," he muttered to himself before returning to the call.

"And what are those?" she asked

Flesh slid further along his length with more force as he continued to review the plans with his caller. "N-now, uh, which one sounds best?" Before she could answer, Art silenced his phone and sat back, rolling his hips forward. *Oh, I hope quality doesn't get this call.*

"Did you hear that, young man?"

"I'm sorry, Suzi, what was that?" *Fuck.* The pace between his legs picked up and Art squirmed more in his seat. The otter bit his tongue to hold back another vocalization.

"I said I want to talk to my husband before we make any changes, but I'm leaning towards that plan with more minutes."

"T-That sounds good. What I'll do is notate your account and you can call us back for any of the same offer, alright?" Art typed away, tripping over his fingers as he made notes.

"Wonderful. I'll talk with him tonight and call back. Is there any way I can talk with you again?" she asked.

Art shook his head. "N-no ma'am. But every other representative h-has the same tools and can see my notes. They'll know exactly what to do." *Please get off my line.*

"Oh, all right." She sighed. "Thank you for all your help, today."

The otter mute the phone again. *I'm getting close.* "Of course. And from everyone here, we hope you have a great day, Suzi." Before he could reply, Art silenced the line. And as if on cue, the lips pulled off, leaving him hard and pent up. *That fucker.*

Taking off his headset, Art stared at the jumbled letters that made up his notes on the screen. *What the hell was she interested in, again?*

"Everything okay, Art?" a floor-walker asked as he passed the otter's desk.

He looked over his shoulder. "Hmm? Uh, yeah. Why?"

"We heard a few sounds coming from over here and got a little worried. Thought you were letting her get to you or something. Just remember, once they're off your line, you never have to talk to them again." She clapped the otter on the shoulder. "Don't let her bother you."

Art nodded. "Yes ma'am, I'll keep that in mind." *Lucas is gonna get me in trouble today...*

The otter typed away, staring at the screen.

"Hey Art," Dennis called as he slid up to the cubicle.

"Afternoon, Boss."

The snow leopard leaned against the cubicle wall. "You on a call?"

"Nope. Once I'm done with my notes, I plan to go into 'meeting.'"

"Sounds good." Dennis clapped Art on the shoulder. "So you know how I've been having you lead these sessions to get you ready for something bigger?"

"Yeah." Art nodded without looking.

"Good news: that 'something bigger' is happening today."

"How so?" The otter took off his headset and turned to face his team lead.

Dennis grinned. "Mike said he's going to make time to be at our meeting today."

The otter's small ears fell. "I thought the CCM was too occupied with the client's visit?"

Dennis' whiskers fell. "Mike likes to show his newest team leads off. You don't sound as excited about this as I thought you would."

Art swallowed. "Well, remember how I said that thing you were talking with Lucas about could be interesting?"

"Yeah?"

The otter looked around before making eye contact with Dennis again. "I may know more about the device than I let on." He pressed a paw over his crotch and squeezed.

Dennis' white tail went limp and his jaw fell. "Shit. Are you kidding me?" he hissed. Art shook his head. "Can you take it off?"

"Not in the time we have before the meeting."

"Ah, hell." Dennis set his paws on his hips. "Mike's already over there, too. Wheel the white board over and pray Lucas doesn't get paws-y *now*." Without another word, Dennis forced up his ears and whiskers, and walked over to his station.

Or worse. Art sighed. *Well, things just got even more interesting.* Grabbing his notepad, the otter pulled the board to the designated area.

He picked up a marker and wrote out the primary metrics while waiting for the others and trying to ignore the well-dressed tiger behind him, and the presence of the toy between his legs. As he got lost in his work and forgot about his fear, a song popped in his head driving him to shake his hips to his own beat.

"You seem energetic today, Art," the tiger said.

The otter shrugged and continued to write. "I always am, sir. Even more so near water." He chirped as he wrote the last number with a flourish and spun around, bobbing his head. Art scanned around the circle. "How are calls going?"

Keeping with the small talk, the otter made an effort to speak with each person as they entered the group. It didn't take long for most of the team to meet up. "Looks like enough of us are here," Dennis said. "Want to get the show on the road and lead us off with averages, Art?"

"I'm not the supervisor here," the otter shrugged with a grin, "but I can do that." As he half-turned to the board, light claws ran across his length, sending a different kind of chill up his spine. Art's ears shot up and he rose up on his toes. *Shit. Of course, now.* He looked from Mike to Dennis. *Well, I guess I'm putting on two kinds of shows at once.*

Forcing a cough into his shoulder, he took a breath and pressed. "Sorry, random chill caught me. Willingness to Recommend is up right now compared to last month by ten-points. With our team at a fifty-two percent, we're leading the call center. So go us." Dennis led the group in a round of applause as he tried to ignore his swelling shaft.

"And, let's make this even better: after fifteen surveys, Charlie leads the center in WTR with an eighty." Art clapped his paws toward a fox at the other side of the circle and everyone else joined in. Charlie's ears lower and tail wrapped around his leg at the praise.

Once the group settled again, Art turned back to the board. "Now while our WTR is great, our First Call Resolution needs a little work." The claws ran from base to tip before stopping, and the otter took a breath. *Thank god.* "We're sitting in fourth place out of seven teams with a forty-" His breath caught in his throat as a soft tongue lapped at him. *Dammit, I hoped he would stop. Then again, not being in control is hot.* He shook his leg, eyes meeting the tigers again. Art's swelling shaft twitched. *Hope he can't tell something's up.* "Sorry. Weather changes have been bothering my knee. Or maybe it's a cold coming on. I can never tell." He cleared his throat. "We have a forty-two and I've got a few tips for the rest of the month."

Art started to flip through his notepad as a slicked-up paw slid along his firm cock. Dropping the notebook, he coughed again in surprise. *Fuck. He wouldn't...*

"Darn frog in my throat," he lied again. Art picked up his legal pad and tried to block out the feeling between his legs by biting the inside of his cheek. "Now, Lucas is our FCR king at a miraculous ninety-four. He said the best way to ensure no one needs to call back is, not only asking the clarifying question but, to probe at every issue that might cause another call."

Once his shaft was slicked up, a paw moved around his sack and his tip pressed against flesh. *Fuck, he is.* Art closed his eyes and leaned against the wall behind him. *Keep it cool.*

"You okay, Boss?" Dennis asked.

Art's ear fell, but he nodded as his tip was surrounded by tightness and warmth. His heart beat faster and his ears warmed in a blush as he stood there, unable to stop what's happening. When that thought ran across his mind, another shiver of excitement ran from tip to tail.

With a long, slow breath he tossed his left leg over his right and flexed his thighs to no relief as he dug his claws into his tail where no one could see. As he locked eyes with the snow leopard, the otter could tell Dennis fought to keep his features still. But never the less, the white tip flicked here and there, nervous. *He knows.*

"Yeah, I'll survive." He forced a smile across his muzzle. "I've been here with the flu before and still got great surveys." From the corner of his eye, the otter saw Mike make a note. *Act normal. Though this is anything but.* Art coughed again, forcing back a squeak of pleasure, before looking at his own legal pad and continued on. "So yeah, every thread. If the caller mentions any sort of service issue, probe into it; if they mention they're thinking of a new phone, probe into it." He looked up at the others around him. "What do you think we should do if the caller mentions they get close to data limits every month?"

"Probe into it," they muttered back.

"Exactly." Art's length was swallowed by the tightness little by little until his sack pressed against flesh. He pinched his tail again, still taking long slow breaths. Never the less his legs shook in anticipation.

"Do you need me to grab you a seat, dude?" Dennis asked.

The otter shook his head. "I'll be good. Just takes a few minutes to pass." He took a step forward, then a step back. "A-a little movement to distract myself." Wiggling his shoulder, he bit back chirps of desire.

"Now for the last metric: everyone's favorite, Customer Satisfaction." He twisted to the board, glancing up at it and back to the group. "Shock and amazement, we're sitting at a solid eighty-three. But we never have an issue with CSat." He shrugged with a grin. "I don't have much more to add. Any questions?" Art scanned the group, forcing his whiskers up. He smiled from person to person, including Mike and Dennis, but no one replied. "In that case, the floor is yours, Dennis." Art raised his paws to the snow leopard.

"Very good. Thank you, Art." He took a step to the center of the circle. "How goes the week, everyone?" he asked as he walked round the group.

As the otter nodded his silent answer, the tightness left most of his cock before returning right away. Art closed his eyes and crossed his arms as a rhythmic pace of pressure slid along his length faster and faster. While he could tell Dennis was talking, it took everything in him to not moan and squeak out loud. *Long slow breaths. Long slow breaths.* He opened his eyes, trying to follow the snow leopard and peak at the tiger. Mike kept his head down as he continued to make notes.

"How's that sound?" Dennis asked with a smile. Everyone else started clapping with excitement and Art joined in late. "Good. Any questions, ladies and gentlemen?"

The pace continued to speed up and Art felt that pressure build. *Damn, I'm getting close.* He closed his eyes again.

Dennis nodded. "Okay then. You guys can go back to your seats." The rest of the team started to walk back. "And remember," Dennis called, "if you have break or lunch scheduled next, take a call first before you go."

The otter stood there, resting against the wall.

"You sure you're okay, Art?" Dennis asked.

"Huh?" The otter opened his eyes with a quick shake of his head. "Oh yeah, sorry." He pushed off the wall and his leg wobbled and he flopped back again.

"Shit dude, take a few extra minutes." Dennis pulled over an empty chair. "Have a seat and don't fall over. We don't want to have to worry about a workman's comp claim," the snow leopard joked. "Must be a real bad knee or cold."

Art chuckled. "Must be." He sat back. "I-I'll just need a few minutes." The pressure stopped sliding as far, but continued to pick up in pace.

Once the rest of the team dispersed, the tiger walked up to him. "You handled yourself well."

The otter bit his cheek before he allowed himself to speak. "T-thank you sir. I try to keep things friendly and bouncy."

"Much like yourself, I see." The tiger chuckled.

Dennis grinned. "You should hear him on the phones. Want to step over here and listen to a few calls?"

Mike nodded. "I think that's a great idea. Care to join us?"

Art shook his head and set a paw over his eyes again. Faster and faster his shaft was surrounded by tightness and warmth. "A-actually, if you don't mind, I think I'm going to catch my breath." A small chirp escaped. "See

47

if I can gather my strength. I won't be long." *Oh damn, I'm close again.* He focused on his breathing and, a moment later, his cock stayed in that pleasured space, squeezing him. With each new pulse around his shaft, the tightness tried to engulf him further, then stopped. Art's dick twitched again as the thought of the smaller otter climaxing ran through his mind.

He sat there for another half a minute before cold air reached his shaft. The otter sighed out loud. *Of course I don't get to finish,* he scoffed to himself. He set both his paws on the arm of the chair and squeezed in frustration. *I know what I'm doing when I get home.*

With one last sigh, he picked himself up. As the recorded call ended, Art cleared his throat. "I think I'm good now. If you have any questions about the calls, let me know."

The tiger nodded. "I can think of a few questions for you. Why don't you and Dennis come to my office for a little bit."

The otter smiled. "I'd love to."

Art had been distracted throughout the rest of his work day and was rock hard on the drive home. *Of course, there're no other issues.* He unlocked the front door and walked in to the apartment. "Honey, I'm home."

Silence answered him.

He dropped his keys and wallet by the door before he took off his shirt and left it where it landed. Walking into the living room, Art found Lucas on the couch, naked and lying on his stomach, arm over his eyes.

He leaned closer to the smaller otter and stroked his cheek. "Lucas, dear, where is it?"

His lover smiled, not moving. "I don't know what you're talking about."

"Really now?" He stood up and unbuckled his slacks, letting them drop to the floor. At the center of his jock was a silver bulge, like a cup. Art reached between his legs, pressing a small button, and a responding chirp came from the bathroom. He shook his head. "Of course you were playing in there."

Standing on the edge of the tub was his cock, suctioned to the porcelain and a small bottle of lube. "Riding me, were you?"

"A little." Lucas grinned.

Art grabbed the bottle and, little by little, worked himself free before returning to the living room.

"So, let me get this straight—"

"Isn't that hard for you?" Lucas smiled.

The larger otter pointed his firm dick at his partner. "You distract me on the way in to work, while on a call, *and* during our meeting—"

"Yes," Lucas raised his arms sleepily, "I was right on the timing."

Art's jaw dropped with a chuckle. "Dammit Lucas."

Lucas curled his arms under his head with a smile. "What I do?"

"You fucked me while I was in a meeting with the call center manager."

"What?" Lucas started to sit up.

"I didn't say you could move. And you don't get to ask questions." A new grin crossed the larger otter's muzzle. "Hell, you didn't let me get off once." Art hit Lucas' rump with his shaft. "You know what, I'm gonna show you how to use this."

The smaller otter raised his ass. "Oh no, anything but that," he said as he wiggled his hips from side to side.

Art made his way behind his lover and raised Lucas' tail. The fur there was already damp with lube. "Were you waiting for a lesson?" Lucas pushed back in reply. "Well, I guess I shouldn't keep you waiting."

With no form or finesse, he shoved himself balls deep into his lover and both otters chirped in pleasure.

THE BR'ER NECESSITIES
BANWYNN OAKSHADOW

Br'er Fox eyed the wriggling burlap sack and danced with glee, "I gots ya now, Br'er Rabbit! I's finally caughts ya!" He laughed and chortled and *poke-poked* at his bundle with a sharp, foxy finger.

Inside the sack, Br'er Rabbit was having trouble believing that Br'er Fox had finally done up an cetched him well an' proper. He tried to ponder a way out of the predikamet he was in.

"What's I gonna do?", he mumbled to hisself, "Mebbe if'n he thinks I yam dead, he'll get bored an' go away."

No sooner had he thunk this thought than he gave a pitiful gasp, a rasping gurgle, and collapsed into the bottom of the bag.

Br'er Fox, having been tricked many, many time by the wily Br'er Rabbit, at first ignored the sudden silence coming from the now still bag.

After a bit, he poked the bag with a finger, "I knows yer in der Br'er Rabbit. I can feels ya. Now you stop all that layin' about and makes some noise in dere!"

Silence.

The fox picked up a long stick and jabbed the bag sharply, trying to bring some response.

Br'er Rabbit winced in pain and stifled a gasp, but mostly managed to remain still and quiet. Yessir, he was one dead bunny.

Now truly worried that he may have scared his quarry to death, Br'er Fox began to very carefully untie the opening of the bag. Though he was right worried, he was determined not to be tricked yet again and watched for the slightest sign of movement. Inside the bag, Br'er Rabbit waited for his chance. As soon as the bag opened, Br'er Rabbit launched himself with his powerful hind legs, feeling them dig and push as he sped for the daylight showing at the mouth of the sack. Nose and ears rocketed to freedom...when the bag clamped firmly closed over his shoulders, trapping him securely. Br'er Rabbit sighed as he realized that Br'er Fox he had well and truly caught him this time.

"Ya's caughts me, Br'er Fox. I gives ma'self up. I's no match for ya no more. So, what'cha gonna do wiff me nows ya caughts me?"

Br'er Fox smiled down at the captive bunny, helpless in his paws, "I's gonna eats ya. What'cha think I's gonna do wiff'n the likes o' you?" He began to drool at the thought of tasty rabbit in the pot.

"Eats me?" squeaked Br'er Rabbit. He thought of games he used to play with the other bunnies when he lived at home with eighteen brothers. Another plan begun to formin' in his head, "Why thank ye, Br'er Fox. That be mighty kind of ye. Here all dis time I thought you meant me harm, but turns out ya wants to eat me. Open dis here bag an' get to eatin'. I's in the mood to get eaten' real good! Mebbe two, three times."

Br'er Fox was right confuzzeled by Br'er Rabbit's excitement and was, for justa moment, taken back. 'Specting trickery, he said, "Gets on down der in dat bag! I's gonna takes ya home and eats ya up der."

Br'er Rabbit squeaked, "All da way home? Dat's good! You take me to yer home...all da way on da other side o' the wood. Ah certainly wouldn't wants ya to eat me here. It's way too open here to gets eaten all proper like."

Br'er Fox was sure he was being tricked by Br'er Rabbit, "Ah, no ya don't! I's on to your tricksy ways. You wants time whilst I takes ya home ta gets free. Well, tain't gonna happen. I's gonna eats ya right here. Now you gets down in dat bag while I gets me some wood for a fire."

"A fire? It's a warm day. Da sun is shinin' bright. Why you wants a fire?"

"Ta cooks ya over, so's I can eats ya!", said Br'er Fox.

"Cook me? Why you wanna do that? How you gonna enjoy eatin' me if'n you cooks me first?"

The fox asked, "What's you mean, Br'er Rabbit? How else am I supposed ta eats ya?"

The wily bunny waited a long bit afore he answered, "Ya mean ya don' know? No one ever showed you the special ways to eats someone? I didn't know. Well, dem's secret ways...so better I jes shut my mouf an let you go on an do it your way."

Br'er Fox had fairly caught Br'er Rabbit and the captor figgered dat meant the bunny's secrets too, "What you talkin' 'bout, Br'er Rabbit? What other ways are der ta eats someone?"

"Ah cain't tell you, Br'er Fox. Dem ways is secret! Ah

never should have said nuffin 'bout dem."

Br'er Fox grabbed the stick that he had used to poke the bag with earlier, "You tell me 'bout dem secret eatin ways or I's gonna hit you wiff dis here stick till ya telz me!"

"Promise you won't tell a livin' soul 'bout these secret eatin ways?"

The fox growled and drooled at the same time, "Ah promise. But, it better not be no trick!"

A meek voice answered, "Okay, I'll teach you how to eat someone real special like, but ah gots ta show ya. It cain't be told real well. It's a showin' kind of thing."

"If you tries to get away, Br'er Rabbit, I'll hit you wiff dis stick and cook you right here! You hear me?"

"I won't try to get away, Br'er Fox. Ah promise. You can keep aholt o' my foot. I don' need it ta show you the eatin' ways."

Br'er Fox carefully lowered the bag around Br'er Rabbit, always being sure to have a good grip on the tricky bunny. Finally, the rabbit was out of the bag, one large hind paw grasped in Br'er Fox's paws, "Now show me these eatin ways!"

Br'er Rabbit looked up at Br'er Fox and slowly scooted hisself between the fox's legs. He gulped a little as his eyes took in the size of his captor's testicles in their white, downy ballsac and the long, furry sheath crawling from it up his belly. Resigning himself to the inevitable, he stuck out his tongue and licked slowly up Br'er Fox's scrotum from his puckered anus to the base of his sheath.

Br'er Fox jumped at the totally unexpected lick and quickly pulled the rabbit away from his bits before they could be eaten,

"Hey der, Br'er Rabbit! What you think you is doin'

down dere? You ain't gonna eat my private parts! I's startin da fire. Get back in dat bag!"

"Hold on jes' one minute, Br'er Fox. Dis ain't eatin like you mean. Dis is a special eatin. More like tastin you might say. An' yo big ole balls sho am tasty! Didn't it feel good when I tasted yer balls?"

Br'er Fox thought about it a minute. He was sure that he could not trust the rabbit, but the lick sure had felt wunnerful good. Maybe jes a little more tastin...then he could put the rabbit back in the bag, "Jes tastin'? Okay, you can taste on me a little bit more, but if'n you try anything else, I is cookin' you up!"

Br'er Rabbit smiled up at his foxy captor and buried his pink nose back between the red, furry thighs and began slurping away at the soft ballsac with his tiny tongue. He placed a paw under the balls to lift and roll them while he lapped away. His other paw rubbed at the base of Br'er Fox's sheath where he could already feel a swelling growin'. He was a little shooked-up. This up close an' all personal-like, the fox's pecker shur looked a might bigger 'en he'd counted on. But, it were too late to change course now.

Ducking his head under the fox's scrotum, he licked daintily around the pink rim of the fox's crinkled winker. He was rewarded by a loud sigh and the spreading of the fox's legs.

Br'er Fox moaned under the bunny's oral ministrations. Warm, tinglin's was washin up an down his spine, fillin' his head. These feelin's way more'n than de ones he got when he stroked his own sheath.

When he felt the rabbit's tongue ringing round his tailhole, Br'er Fox quivered and arched his back, pulling the bunny in closer.

"Oh my, Br'er Rabbit! Dat sho am some mighty fine

tastin' yo am doin! But look at dis. Yo is makin' mah fur all wet an' sticky. You better be ready to clean up dis mess yo am makin'."

Br'er Rabbit looked up to see what Br'er Fox was talking about and saw three or so inches of slick, pink foxcock protruding from his sheath an' drippin' steadily onta his belly. The rabbit wasn't sure if he could handle the fox's larger cock, but realized that the options was worse. Placing both paws in the fox's thighs, he raised hisself until he was leaning over the furry sheath and shiny cock. His little, fuzzy balls rested against the fox's as he leaned down and lapped the seeping tip of the vulpine prick. As the taste and smell of the foxy cock filled his head, he found that he was beginning to enjoy things himself. Steeling himself, he opened his mouth wide and took the tip of Br'er Fox's cock into it, sucking gently, feeling dribbles of vulpine precum sliding down his throat.

"Oh yes! Dat am sho good, Br'er Rabbit. Yo is a good taster. Taste my cock, Br'er Rabbit! Taste my cock real good now!", He grasped the rabbit's ears and pulled his head inexorably down as he pushed his hips up until the tip of his cock was pressed firmly against the roof of Br'er Rabbit's mouth at the back of his throat. Br'er Fox could force no more in but still half his foxness stood exposed between the bunny's nose and his own belly.

Br'er Rabbit struggled as he felt the too large cock being forced ever deeper into his mouth. He began gagging and found it nearly impossible to breathe. Unable to lick or suck, he concentrated only in surviving the assault.

The fox pulled the rabbit off of his aching prick, "Why did yo stop tastin', Br'er Rabbit? Is this some kind o' trick? You taste it good now!"

"I cain't, Br'er Fox. Yo cock is too big for po l'il me to get all in my mouf. Mebbe if'n I as to get up on yo' belly it could go in a might easier."

Concentrating more now on the building pressure in his cock than in the possible escape of the rabbit, he nodded and lifted the bunny and settled him on his belly with his fuzzy tail staring the fox in the face while the rabbit's mouth once again began suckling at the tip of the fox's cock.

"Ooooooooooooh! Dat am nice! Here, you open wide an taste more o' this fox!" He slowly arched his hips and began sliding more of his cock into the rabbit's mouth.

Br'er Rabbit felt his throat being forced open as the pulsing cock slid ever deeper into him. Grunting around the dripping organ he managed to pant through his nose as he felt hot, salty liquid spurting at the back of his throat. The fox's watery precum eased the passage of his eager cock and soon Br'er Rabbit's nose was pushing the fox's furry sheath back to the very base of his cock. It felt as if Br'er Fox's cock was going right through him and that the fox must surely be cumming directly into his belly. Helpless now, and no longer sure this plan was such a good one, he could only swallow urgently to keep from drowning in foxy seed, his throat milking even more of the salty fluid from the tool in question in the process.

"Unh! Mmmmmmmmmm! Dat's so good, Br'er Rabbit. Unnnhhh! Yo is slurpin' me mighty fine." Br'er Fox grunted and began to withdraw a bit from the rabbit's stretched mouth and slide it back in. Each stroke increased the building pressure that was mounting at the base of his balls and working its way up his spine. He grabbed one of Br'er Rabbit's hind legs in each paw and lifted them in the air to hold the bunny at an angle that made it easier to pump himself into the hot, little mouth.

"Sssssooooo tight, Mister Bunny. I ain't never knew nuthin' could feel this good!"

Br'er Rabbit had no answer, being busy trying to keep from suffocating on the big dick lodged in his throat. Panic began to mount as he felt the fox thrusting into him and watched as the knot at the base of Br'er Fox's cock began to swell and push against his nose.

Br'er Fox panted and moaned as he humped his hips into his helpless captive's mouth. Looking down he realized for the first time what sort of view afforded itself with the rabbit's hind legs lifted and spread that way. He looked carefully between the bunny's legs as he continued to hunch away. The bunny had little fuzzy balls, held up much closer to his body that the fox's own and Br'er Fox could not immediately discern a sheath on the little rabbit. Finally, he realized that the small bulge and tiny opening in front of the bunny's balls must be the sheath. Under the twitching, cottonball tail he saw a tiny, pink, puckered opening.

"Hmmmm...' thought Br'er Fox, "I wunners if tastin someone feels as good as gettin tasted do?"

Continuing to hump himself steadily into the bunny's mouth, he leaned forward and licked between the rabbit's legs just to see what it tasted like. Musky and salty, but mighty tasty. He liked the way it felt when his tongue lifted Br'er Rabbit's balls and slid over them. He felt a sharp little nub run across his tongue as he lapped a second time and realized that he must be forcing the bunny cock out into the open. Slurping with gusto now, he drew his tongue again and again between the bunny's legs, slow then fast, hard then feather light. Soon Br'er Rabbit quit struggling to push away from the fox's cock and began to wriggle himself against the broad, wet vulpine tongue slathering hungrily between his thighs. Br'er Fox felt a spurt of wetness trickle down his throat and then another. As the rabbit ground himself against his tongue, the fox realized that Br'er Rabbit was a'cummin in his mouth.

Pulling his head back, he looked once again between the rabbit's legs where a now fully exposed pink cock glistened with saliva. The bunny prick was larger than Br'er Fox had expected and was still spurting quick jets of white, bunny cum. He stuck out his tongue and caught the rest of it, rolling it in his mouth and tasting it carefully.

He grunted as his own cock threatened to burst. "Oh! Oh! Unh! I likes dis special eatin! Now eats dis fox cock, Br'er Rabbit!"

Br'er Rabbit was no longer panicking. The fox tongue slavering between his legs had caught him by surprise and brought him quickly to and over the brink of a very nice climax. Now, he used his throat to milk the cock lodged there, actually hungry for a taste of the fox's spunk. Hips humping against Br'er Fox's tongue and his own head grinding desperately into the fox's crotch, he gulped and slurped for all he was worth.

"OOOoooooooo! Dis is it! Ah is gonna cum! Ah's gonna shoot my dick in yo mouf, Br'er Rabbit" with these words, Br'er Fox humped himself hard into the rabbit, forcing his swelling knot past the bunny's lips and into the tight embrace of that hungry maw. Even as he sank himself fully, he felt surge after surge gushing up from the base of his cock to pour into the bunny's throat, "Oh yeah! Drink dat fox cum! Suck dat dick! Uhhhhnnnnnn!"

Br'er Fox's hips slowed as his knot swelled to its

fullest dimensions and his climax settled into a steady, rhythmic spurting of his seed into the rabbit's mouth. He noticed Br'er Rabbit humping at the air where his foxy tongue had been a short time before and panted while he watch the pink cock swinging between those soft, fluffy thighs. He leaned close and began to lick happily at the cock and balls before his nose. After only a few seconds he felt Br'er Rabbit quiver and was rewarded with another small load of cum.

This time he did not stop but continued lapping, pausing only to lick at the rabbit's tightly clamped hole as Br'er Rabbit had done to him. In less than ten minutes, the rabbit came six more times before his cock finally grew soft and withdrew back into its sheath despite anything Br'er Fox could do to keep it out and hard. Realizing that his swollen knot in the rabbit's mouth held Br'er Rabbit more securely than mere paws ever could, he lowered the bunny back to his belly and leaned back to enjoy the sensations of the a hot throat milking at his cock, harvesting every spurt of his fox cum as fast as he could produce it.

Yessir, Br'er Fox was mighty glad that he had finally caught Br'er Rabbit.

Flat on his back, hands tucked under his head and a rabbit sucking hungrily on his still spurting pecker. That's how Br'er Bear found the two enemies when he happened to amble into the meadow. He scratched at his head as he stared at the curious scene before him and tried to make sense of it. From the smile on Br'er Fox's muzzle, it shor looked as he was likin' whatever it was that Br'er Rabbit was doing to him. He cocked his head and looked at the bunny gulping away at Br'er Fox's crotch. Br'er Rabbit's cheeks bulged hugely and his throat was swollen. He swallowed almost constantly and panted loudly through his twitching pink nose. But he had this dreamy kinda look in his eyes showin' that he was glad of what was goin' on.

It didn't make a lick of sense so Br'er Bear ambled his way to where the two were doin' whatever it was that they was doin', "My now, but if'n this ain't truly a strange sight to behold. What is y'all doin', Br'er Fox?"

"I's finally caughts Br'er Rabbit," crowed Br'er Fox, "An now I is fixin' to eat him."

Br'er Bear looked that the pulsing cock sunk in the rabbit's mouth and replied, "Looks more like Br'er Rabbit issa eatin you, Br'er Fox. Don' that hurt?"

"Oh no, Br'er Bear! Dis don' hurt at all. It shor feels good...an dat's the truth. I ain't supposed to tell no one, but seein' as you is lookin' at it right now, I reckon I can tell you. This is a special kind of eatin'."

Now Br'er Bear liked eating more than about anything in the whole world, so this talk of a special kind of eating peaked his interest, even if he could not quite figure out what this special eating could do to fill an empty belly.

"Tell me 'bout dis 'special eatin', Br'er Fox. Ah is mighty hungry."

Br'er Fox membered how Br'er Rabbit had splained it an' said, "Well, it's a showin kind of thing so you stan' right here behind me and I'll show you how I eats Br'er Rabbit."

With that, he once again lifted Br'er Rabbit's hind legs, spreading them very wide to give Br'er Bear the best view possible, and slowly licked under the bunny's tail until his bright shiny cock poked its way from its furry sheath. When the little cock was fully exposed, he lifted the rabbit a little higher and wrapped his muzzle around the morsel and suckled like a pup at the teat.

Soon Br'er Rabbit was pounding like a woodpecker on a grub tree into Br'er Fox's mouth, moaning around the member still locked solidly in his mouth. His fluffy tail twitched as he quickly came two more times into the fox's mouth before his cock once again shrunk and refused to respond to any more licks or sucks.

Br'er Fox lowered the rabbit back to his belly and opened his mouth, exposing the pearly white pool of bunny cum coating his tongue. Making sure that Br'er Bear had seen it, he swallowed the load of spunk slowly, savoring the taste and feel of it as it slid warmly down his throat.

"Br'er Rabbit don' give a whole lot at one time, but he sho do give it a whole bunch o' times. I is still on my first an' he has already spurted into me a whole mess o' times."

Br'er Bear had watched the obvious relish with which Br'er Fox had swallowed Br'er Rabbit's cum and decided that this was something he had to explore, "Let me have Br'er Rabbit for a bit, frien' fox, so as I can have some o' this special eatin' too."

"Well, Br'er Bear, it's like this. Br'er Rabbit can' do no mo' till he has rested some. An you couldn't have him no way anyhow cause he is stuck on my cock right good an' bound to stay there awhile. I is fillin his belly right up wif my foxy seed.", so saying, he poked a little at Br'er Rabbit's belly so that Br'er Bear could hear the sloshing of the bunny's cum filled stomach.

"You mean that bein' tasted feels good too? Yo likes what Br'er Rabbit is doin' to you?", asked Br'er Bear.

"Oh yes, Br'er Bear. Tastin' is mighty fun and ah likes doin it, but gettin' tasted on...dat is wunnerful! I ain't never felt nuthin' so good afore in my whole life! Ah has been like dis in Br'er Rabbit's mouth fo the longest time and it feels so good I never want to stop."

Br'er Bear danced, "Well get dat rabbit off'n you so's I can feel dat tastin'!"

"Ah cain't till da swellin go down, and dis here rabbit sucks so good dat it might take a long time afore that happens."

Br'er Bear scratched his head some more while he thought. Br'er Fox an' Br'er Rabbit looked to be havin' a right good time from the looks of things. He stood and scratched and pondered as he tried to figure a way for him to get some of this special eatin' too.

"Br'er Fox, you say dat rabbit is all done an' cain't do no more fer abit?", said Br'er Bear.

"Dat's a fact, Br'er Bear. He done squirted so much juice dat he might jes be done fer all day."

In dat case, I am sho you won' mind if'n I take his place.", whereupon Br'er Bear stepped around to straddle Br'er Fox with a foot on either side of his hips, Br'er Rabbit still sucking and gulping under him, and his groin inches from the fox's nose.

Br'er Fox licked his muzzle as he looked at the furry crotch in his face and smelled the deep, masculine musk of the big bear. Two round balls, each bigger than both of Br'er Fox's clenched fists, rolled in a heavy sack that begged to be licked. Above those balls, a sheath somewhere between Br'er Rabbit's and his own in appearance but much, much larger than any he had ever seen before bobbed back and forth as Br'er Bear shifted, waiting to see what Br'er Fox would do.

Br'er Bear was not sure what to expect. It sure looked like the two was havin' lots of fun, but he didn't understand why. He wondered what the white stuff Br'er Rabbit had put in Br'er Fox's mouth was and why Br'er Fox seemed to like the taste of it so much. You see,

Br'er Bear was not an adventurous sort and had never even explored what was in his own sheath, so did not know what kinds of pleasures it could bring. He stood there, shifting nervously from paw to paw while he waited for Br'er Fox to start tastin' him.

Now that he was face to face--so to speak--with Br'er Bear's private parts, Br'er Fox had a pretty good idea how Br'er Rabbit had felt not too long ago. Using both paws, he reached out and gently cupped the bear's huge balls and fondled them slowly. He felt their heaviness roll back and forth, squeezing them just a little and then rolling them some more. After just a few seconds, Br'er Bear shifted to widen his stance a little and Br'er Fox stuck out his tongue to lick up and around the bruin's fuzzy scrotum. He was rewarded by a loud gasp and a deep rumble of pleasure.

The big bear grunted and groaned as his balls were rolled in the fox's nimble fingers. He spread his legs without realizing it to give Br'er Fox easier access to his most private parts. He almost passed out when a soft, wet tongue washed over his scrotum and then plunged between his legs to slaver his entire groin in hot breath and saliva.

Br'er Fox found the taste of bear to be immensely pleasing. Better even than bunny. Thinking of the rabbit, he reached down a paw to stroke the soft fur of the rabbit's back while his aching nuts gave up yet another dribble of watery cum to Br'er Rabbit's insatiable throat. Sticking his muzzle just under Br'er Bear's legs, he looked up at the winking hole just under the bear's stumpy tail. He plunged his tongue at the hole without preamble. The attack took the bear totally by surprise and his tongue slid in quite deeply before the sphincter clamped down on it.

Br'er Bear yelped and almost pulled away, "What's you doin' down der, Br'er Fox? Is did more of dat special tastin? Ooooooh! Dat feels funny, but it feels right nice, too!", as he loosened up his ass and the fox's tongue began to wriggle, he sighed and spread his legs even further, growling deep in his chest. He barely noticed that his cock had begun to grow and slide from his sheath.

Br'er Fox slurped away at the bear's tail hole, pushing his tongue up there as far as it would go and swirling it around. His paws mauled the bruin's balls, rolling and squeezing them as he sucked and licked at the big bear's ass. He felt something brushing the top of his head between his ears and looked up to see an enormous cock extending from Br'er Bear's sheath to hang in the air, bobbing with each beat of his heart. Even as he watched, the massive organ grew larger and stiffer, purple veins pulsing along its length. A large drop of clear liquid glistened at the very tip of the huge pole.

Br'er Fox took a deep breath and slid his muzzle over the fat head of the bear's prick, feeling it slide along his tongue and probe the back of his throat. This was much different than licking and sucking the much smaller rabbit and the inexperienced fox was soon gagging and pulling back.

Still, the wonderful taste and feel of a hard, fat cock in his mouth drew him to try again. Taking it slower and easier this time, he was able to take a bit more of Br'er Bear's shaft into his mouth and keep it there.

Br'er Bear whimpered as he felt his cock engulfed in a warm, moist mouth for the first time. Looking down he could hardly believe his eyes as he watched half his length disappear into Br'er Fox's mouth. His balls immediately tightened as did his chest. Breathing in short gasps, he tried to come to terms with the intense feelings washing through him.

Br'er Rabbit heard and felt the slurping and rocking as Br'er Fox began sucking on Br'er Bear's fat pole. He had known that canines 'tied' and that he would be here for a while, but he marvelled at just how long the fox had been cumming. His poor belly was bloated with salty spunk and his jaws ached from being forced open for so long. Still, it was rather exciting and having the bear getting sucked off for the first time in his life right above him excited him even more. He began to push his hips against the silky fur of the fox's belly, still damp from his dripping precum earlier.

Very quickly his own cock was fully erect and gliding through the wonderful mixture of fur and seed.

Br'er Fox slowly became accustomed to having the bear's large cock wedged in his mouth and began to bob his head back and forth, slowly taking more and more into him with each stroke. He felt Br'er Rabbit humping against him and the rocking sent new surges of pleasure through his own cock and he too began humping back against the rabbit.

Br'er Bear could never have been prepared for what was happening to him. He felt a tingling pressure building at the base of his cock and tried to squeeze it back as it grew stronger and stronger with each slurp on his cock.

"Stop, Br'er Fox! I cain't help it. If'n you don' stop now, I is gonna pee in yo mouf!," he cried as the need for release grew even more urgent.

Br'er Rabbit moaned around the fox's knot as yet another climax rippled through him. One benefit of being a rabbit he thought...they is almost always ready for just one more. Even now he could feel another one building as his cum mixed with the fox's in the deep fur of the belly under him.

Br'er Fox heard Br'er Bear's plea and responded by sucking even harder and by sliding a paw between the bear's legs to tickle his winker with a finger. Soon he decided that that may have been a mistake.

Br'er Bear felt the pressure build to where he no longer cared where he found release as long as he found it soon. Snarling, he grabbed a red ear in each paw and shoved his engorged cock deep into the fox's mouth. Grunting, he humped himself again and again, pushing himself as deeply as he could go.

Br'er Fox was choking but ecstatic. Held helpless by the large bear he also shared the feeling raging through him. His back arched as a final wave of semen spewed from his cock into Br'er Rabbit's mouth even as the rabbit spurted yet again onto his belly.

Br'er Bear threw back his massive head and roared as his first orgasm tore through him. Gripping so tightly that he almost crushed the poor fox's head, he ground his crotch into Br'er Fox's muzzle as thick, gooey strands of jism fountained from his cock. When Br'er Fox managed to pull back, Br'er Bear was still cumming and soon the fox's face was covered with sticky, white rivulets of semen. Finally, panting and quivering, Br'er Bear took two weak steps to the side and flopped to the ground with a dazed look in his eyes and a semi-hard cock leaking a tiny trail of cum into the grass.

Br'er Fox began to catch his breath and lick at his face, trying to find every tasty drop of bear cum. He did not realize that his knot had subsided until Br'er Rabbit popped free and sped off, leaving him with his belly fur well drenched in cum as well.

Br'er Rabbit stopped near the edge of the clearing and licked at his own muzzle and rubbed his very full belly happily. He heard Br'er Fox holler weakly at him.

"I'll catch you again, Br'er Rabbit! Jes you don wait an see if'n I don' catch you again! I's gonna teach you to trick me!"

Br'er Rabbit chuckled. He was sure that Br'er Fox would try very, very hard to catch him again...and he had a feeling that he just may succeed real soon. He hopped into the bushes surrounding the clearing and realized that he was getting hard again thinking of showing Br'er Fox about the other fun places a nice hard cock could be put.

GIFT OF THE GODDESS
MOG MOOGLE

Bartelmeu rubbed his forehead and groaned. Looking over his court, he saw the attendants making everything perfect for the day. The hearth fire kindled to life and the carpet from the entrance to his dais pulled tight. As expected, he kept up appearances.

Though he had not heard the first petitioner of the day, fatigue and stress already troubled the king. He was grateful that his first audience would not be a subject with a problem, but his southern ally.

"Announcing his highness, Prince Arhon of Melath," the herald announced as attendants opened the doors of the Grand Hall.

The lion stood up from his throne as a raccoon in ornate silk clothing and a roundlet hat with a large peacock plume entered. He was followed by two armor-clad bodyguards. Behind them was a female mouse in a modest robe. She appeared out of place traveling with the lavish prince.

Half way to the king the bodyguards stopped, but the female servant kept following. When he arrived at the base of the dais, he removed his hat and he and his servant both knelt.

"Arhon," Bartelmeu said as he walked down the steps. "Rise. You know you don't have to kneel to me."

The prince chuckled as he stood up. "Not all monarchs are as informal as you, my friend."

"I have no doubt that I would still be a prince, if the gods hadn't determined otherwise."

"But you've done well enough as king." Prince Arhon put his hat back on and adjusted it. "Even if it's one of the less profitable stops on the Tradeway, Liborg still is the most pleasant."

"Now you sound like my counselors. Wealth is more than the coins in your coffers."

"I can't entirely disagree," he said as he looked back at his servant, still kneeling. "I have something for you. Consider it a wedding gift, since my father and I will be occupied during the Goddess Festival."

Bartelmeu's eyes widened and he looked around to make sure none of his court attendants were in earshot. "That was finalized just this morning. There are only two advisers that even know of that. How could you possibly—"

"Don't worry, it was none of your advisers."

Bartelmeu furled his brow at the prince. "That's not what I would call reassuring."

"Your northern rival surrounds himself with less scrupulous individuals solely for the benefit of adoration." Arhon clicked his tongue and then smiled at the king. "But his daughter is lovely. Marriage to

Princess Ivette seems a fine way to end the troubles."

"Binding myself away to end the conflict that killed my father is not what I would consider fine." Bartelmeu sighed and shook his head. "The same king that took my father seven years ago barters his child away for some trade concessions when the war he started gets too expensive? It's reprehensible."

"My friend, I know it may seem so. Consider this, though; before your twentieth summer, you've ensured peace in a way your father or his father never could."

"I often wonder how you maintain your levity." Bartelmeu rubbed his brow and sighed.

"Do you? Well then, let's discuss your gift."

Bartelmeu looked at the mouse as Prince Arhon motioned for her to rise. She approached the two but kept a respectable distance with her eyes focused on the ground.

"You know slavery is illegal in my lands," the king said in a stern voice as he folded his arms.

"It's well and good that she's not a slave then, eh?" Arhon said and cocked his eyebrow.

Bartelmeu scowled.

"Listen, my friend," Arhon began as he eased Bartelmeu around with their backs to her. "I understand your feelings about this particular market, but would you even know what to do with a woman?"

"That is outrageous!" Bartelmeu furled his brow as his tail lashed under the cloak. With a quick glance around, he leaned in toward the prince. "Just what are you insinuating?"

"That you have been too busy being a good king to enjoy the brothels, of course. She was trained at the largest brothel in Melath. They specialize in being discreet for clients that don't necessarily want anyone to know they use their services."

"So, you are trying to gift me a brothel wench?"

"Sire?" the mouse said.

Bartelmeu turned back around and watched as she looked up from the ground. Her eyes still wouldn't meet his, but even as she looked at his chest, he could see a determined glint in her exotic violet irises.

"I beg pardon for overhearing, sire, but I can assure I'm unsullied by any man."

He cocked an eyebrow as he looked her over. "I'm sorry, miss, but that seems unlikely if you were purchased from a brothel. Honestly, owning another as property is the chief concern."

"Highness, putting aside my servitude for the moment; I can tell you that I've been trained in recognizing needs and desires. I've been tutored by masters in the art since I was young. I was brought up to serve nobility or royalty."

"You see?" Arhon said as he nudged Bartelmeu with his elbow. "You may trust her to be discreet, and you'll learn how to properly keep your new bride firmly in your bed."

"Arhon, I have no desire to own a slave, let alone one for carnal pleasure."

"Sire?" she spoke up again. Her eyes lifted from his chest. "I am deeply humbled by your concern for me. If you do not wish to own me as property, please allow me to at least serve as an attendant to you."

Bartelmeu's tail twitched under the cloak. "You are insistent I accept this gift. I suspect this as an attempted infiltration."

"Nothing of the sort," Prince Arhon said. "There's no need for subterfuge with you, my friend. You make all your feelings clear. I assure you, on behalf of myself, my father and our kingdom, this is a genuine gift. To celebrate a long needed peace between all our peoples and our less cordial northern compatriots."

"The duplicity of merchants and traders has never been made more evident." Bartelmeu shook his head. "I trust you as a friend, but when it comes to state affairs you will understand if I am wary of odious motives."

"You wouldn't be a king if you trusted everything at face value, my friend." Arhon chuckled and shook his head. "In four days, I will be returning on the Tradeway from Sovia. If you're still unsatisfied with your gift, I will return her to Melath."

Bartelmeu grumbled and looked down at his *gift* again. Her eyes locked with his. The forced shyness of a slave with a broken will was absent, and there was an unusual sternness in its place. A sense of foreboding filled him, but he couldn't grasp the reason. "What is your name?"

"What would you wish it to be, sire?" Her tone was demure.

"No, none of that. If you really want to live in this city and serve as one of my subjects, you will have to learn that the only difference between a royal and common bloodline is the station that the gods put us in at birth."

"I see." Her eyes reflected the glow of the hearth as she looked directly at the king. "My former Mistress called me Silverthorn."

Bartelmeu scowled in disgust.

"Silverthorn will do." She gave the lion a sincere smile.

"Very well. I will have you escorted to the attendants' quarters and assigned a bed. You are not to have access to the archives or the court until I say otherwise."

Silverthorn looked the king up and down before giving him a small bow. "Of course, your highness."

Bartelmeu watched her for a moment before prying his gaze away. He looked at the prince. "I am still wary of this gift, Arhon."

"We will see if you still feel that way on my return trip. Now, if you'll excuse my abrupt departure, we must get moving if we're to make Sovia in two days."

"Gods be with you, friend."

"At least the gods of fortune and fair travel," the raccoon prince said before he turned away and left the Grand Hall with his bodyguards.

Bartelmeu backed up to his throne when the double doors closed behind the prince and his escort. Glancing over toward the rear doors, he saw the mouse escorted by another attendant. She stopped and examined one of the tapestries. The king watched her as she tugged on the material and pulled a wrinkle out of the crest of Liborg embroidered on it.

Silverthorn examined it to make sure that it was in order, and then she looked at the king. Her eyes never lost their determination, and there was a knowing glint in them. The corners of her muzzle curled into a little smile before she resumed following the attendant out of the Grand Hall.

Bartelmeu sat down on his throne as his ears twitched. "What a strange woman," he mused to himself.

The sun dipped below the bailey walls as King Bartelmeu dismissed his final petitioner. Many times he had to remind himself the problems of his subjects were equal to his own. He tugged the front of the cloak away from his neck where sitting on the material had constricted him.

Court attendants were snuffing the torches and braziers. They tended the fire in the large hearth so that it would have embers to rekindle the next morning. Bartelmeu paid little attention to them as he rose from his throne and stepped down. He went to the door at the back of his hall that would lead to the bedrooms.

He noticed the mouse standing by his door. She kept her gaze fixed on him as he approached. The color of her irises gleamed in the soft candlelight of the wall sconces. Bartelmeu furled his brow. He assumed his intent not to bed her hadn't been clear.

"Good evening, sire," she said as she opened the door to his bedroom.

"Good evening," he replied. "I thought you would be assigned elsewhere. There are plenty of attendants for the bedchambers."

"I have an assignment, sire. I'm your personal attendant."

"I am afraid I do not require—" A familiar scent wafted into his nostrils. "Did you use my aromatic oils?"

"I know you're fond of this blend." Her unfaltering stare stayed locked on him. "I heard you have it specially made. It is rather soothing, isn't it?"

"That bath is off limits to all but the Royal Family," Bartelmeu snarled.

"Oh? But Matriarch Tressia gave me permission."

"Miss Silverthorn, I find that very difficult to believe. The head attendant of my keep is most meticulous. She does *not* make exceptions."

"Oh, it wasn't really an exception." Silverthorn's sweet smile faded. "You see, I'm an extension of you. I'm your desires."

Bartelmeu scoffed and shook his head, but her eyes told him an absolute truth. It made the young king falter. He'd looked his enemies in the eyes and never flinched. No mere brothel worker could compare to sovereigns or savages that commanded armies to threaten his people. "No," he said plainly. "Today has been long and trying. I just wish to retire to my bedchamber."

"Of course, sire," she said and bowed her head.

Bartelmeu stepped into his bedroom and stood on the plush handwoven rug. Behind him, the door mechanism latched and he breathed a sigh of relief. He determined to speak to Tressia in the morning to see if the mouse was lying.

His paws moved up to the gem-crested brooch on the royal cloak and he unfastened it. The thick material hung loose on his shoulders while he moved his paws up to rub his eyes. As the tired burn of exhaustion prickled his eyelids, he felt materiel slide off and lift from his body.

Bartelmeu turned around in surprise to see the mouse standing there. He watched in stunned amazement as she held it up and began folding the material.

She took great care to keep it from brushing the floor, treating it with respect. The mouse demonstrated she knew what the symbol of the kingdom meant.

"How dare you handle my father's mantle!" he roared as he readied himself to expel the intruder into his bedroom with his own paws.

"The only difference between you and I, *sire*," her emphasis on the title laced with disrespect, "is the station the gods put us in at birth."

Bartelmeu couldn't contain his rage. His claws bared in anger as he stepped toward her, but her gaze stopped him in his tracks. Her eyes were unrepentant, dour, and unafraid. The king's courage waned at the look of a creature barely half his size. "You...you cannot just—"

"Be silent!" she commanded. She broke her entrancing and terrifying eyes away from the king and patted the cloak with her paw. "This is a thing. It's a piece of cloth that has no meaning if the man wearing it has no power to back it." She glanced back at him with the harshness subdued and smiled. "I know my king has all the authority to rule inside his heart. The gods gifted you with a soul that is strong enough to command a nation. Don't doubt that, and don't ever believe that authority resides anywhere but inside of you."

"Miss Silverthorn?" he said in a hushed voice that almost trembled.

"No, I'm afraid that title won't do. You see, you're strong and powerful, and you've been strong and powerful for so long that it's made you weary. What you want most is to give up some of that power and relish in lack of responsibility." Silverthorn walked to a large armoire with ornate carvings and opened it. She placed the mantle on a shelf embroidered with the royal emblem; its resting place when not on the shoulders of its king. "From now on, when we are behind the closed doors of your bedchamber, you will address me as Mistress."

Bartelmeu cocked an eyebrow as he looked down at the mouse. "I do not think—"

"No," she interrupted, "and that's my gift to you. You don't have to think." Silverthorn approached the king. As soon as he started to recoil, her paw shot up and snatched the collar of his gold trimmed tunic and she pulled his face down to hers, muzzle-to-muzzle. "All you have to do is submit."

Bartelmeu pulled away. His morals and his convictions, his station and dedication to it, the status quo he'd held firm to; all of it told him to resist her. "You presume to know me," he said in an effort to fight against his own thoughts. "But I do not—"

"No, you do not. *I* do." She stepped within reaching distance once more. "I know your desires. Your needs and your dreams. I'm all that you are sheltered from in your station but secretly and desperately want. I am your Mistress. Say it," she instructed.

Bartelmeu swallowed hard, but his resolve stiffened. He was a king, and he would not be dictated to. "This is absurd. You're a brothel wench."

Silverthorn's eyes never broke the king's, and her expression made it clear that she was displeased with his disrespect. She grabbed the collar of his tunic with both paws and yanked downward.

Bartelmeu grabbed her wrists out of instinct, but the little mouse didn't even flinch. His mouth was going dry. He could see the outline of his reflection in her pupils wreathed in her royal purple irises. He tried to close his eyes to avoid her, but a rough jerk on his collar brought it right back to the mouse.

"I am you mistress." She was so close that every breath dampened his whiskers.

"Yes." Bartelmeu's response was quiet and trembled.

"*Yes?* That is how you address the new owner of your body? The one who relieves you of your burdens?"

Bartelmeu's eyes widened. "No, that is not—"

"Say it!" she demanded. She jerked the collar of his tunic so rough that fabric stressing echoed in the large room.

"Yes, Mistress." Bartelmeu's cheeks and ears heated with a combination of humiliation and arousal.

"Good." She released his collar, stepped back and pulled the twine sash loose, letting the front of her robe open. She shrugged it off her shoulders and it crumpled to the floor behind her. It revealed a purple silken shawl arranged on her body in a 'V' shape. Around her wrists were bracelets that looked like rope woven with gold leaf in the twine.

Bartelmeu drank in the features of her slim frame, petite breasts and meticulously groomed white fur. The royal colors of her sash stood in stark contrast. He looked up her body until he stopped at her eyes.

"Strip, little cub," she commanded.

"I..."

"Strip!" Her tone left no question that he had no choice in the matter.

Bartelmeu nodded.

Silverthorn scowled at his silent reply. "When I give you an order, you will respond appropriately and comply immediately."

"Yes, Mistress," Bartelmeu said in a hushed voice as he unbound the ribbon on the neck of his tunic. As soon as it was loose, he peeled it over his head as quick as he could. He rose up from his hunched position that he had maintained since she had forced him eye-level with her. He pulled the sash around his waist free and pushed the fabric of his breeches down, snagging the tip of his exposed arousal before they fell around his ankles.

"Now, let me get a good look." She examined his barbed member for a moment, taking a finger and running a pad along the underside. As it caressed the spines near the glans, Bartelmeu gasped and she chuckled. Taking a moment to examine the fingerpad she had teased him with, she looked up at him with a grin.

"Oh! Look at this," she said as she held her paw up to his face with her index finger raised, pre glistening on the soft pink pad. "You've sullied the body of your Mistress. That will not do. Take care of it."

Bartelmeu looked at the slick clear liquid on her finger and blinked his eyes. He opened his mouth to ask for clarification, but as soon as his did her finger was in it. The lion grimaced and tried to pull away, but the mouse's other paw grabbed his jaw under his chin and held it. It was once more made obvious that there were no choices in the matter.

The musky, alkaline flavor of his own sexual fluid was already sinking into his rough tongue. The thought of licking up something that came out of his maleness, something he'd been taught was a gift from the Goddess for procreation in sacred acts of love, repulsed him.. Worst of all, his manhood throbbed as he was forced to swallow his beliefs.

Silverthorn's finger slipped from his muzzle and she released him. Her expression made it clear that she was not happy with his reluctance.

The lion fidgeted for a moment then splayed his ears back. "Forgive me."

"Oh? So is that genuine regret that you failed to obey my command?"

Bartelmeu looked at the floor as he searched his thoughts for the answer. He wanted to be unrepentant, but the defiance he was seeking was absent. "Yes," he admitted. The sincerity terrified and excited him.

"Yes, what?" she demanded.

"Yes, Mistress," he said as he looked up at her.

"Well, cubs do make mistakes," she said after a moment and then her expression softened. "I will continue my tour. When you're given a command, I trust there won't be a repeat of the last incident."

"No, Mistress."

"Good. Next time you fail to follow an order, you will be punished."

Bartelmeu wondered what being punished would entail as the little mouse walked around him. Her paws caressed down his arm, then over to his sides and the flanks of his rear. The lion's body quivered at the delicate mouse fingers combing through his fur. "Good," she said. "You've taken excellent care of yourself, despite being in a position to partake in excess."

Bartelmeu blushed at the compliment as she moved around to his backside. He didn't dare look over his shoulder at her to see what she was doing. He felt her fingers slide up the back of his thighs and then over his buttocks. The mouse's small foot pressed against his and force his stance wider. Her paws slid up to the base of his tail and when he heard her command lift it, he did without hesitation. She parted the cheeks of his rear.

His foot claws extended and they dug into the rug as he felt his Mistress's breath against his backside. Bartelmeu steadied himself as her nose pressed against him and her whiskers brushed against his fur. Silverthorn's tongue brushed against the texture of his tailhole and Bartelmeu's eyes shot open as he inhaled with sharp gasp.

The claws pierced through to the floor beneath it and gouged the strong hardwood like it was parchment. His knees began to wobble and he almost lost his balance as his eyes rolled up.

Her tongue ceased its gentle strokes and snaked inside him past his tailring. Bartelmeu grunted as he saw black swirling stars through his half closed eyelids. Silverthorn's tongue worked his sensitive opening with practiced skill.

He would doubt her claim of chastity if he could focus on anything other than the unbridled pleasure. Rumors of secret cultist sects of the fertility goddess had such practices, but the actual experience was overwhelming. His breath quickened and his body quivered. As he was at the brink of losing consciousness, she ceased and withdrew her tongue.

Bartelmeu fought with every ounce of his will to stay standing. He was not even aware of the little mouse's movements until his erratic breathing was under control. He forced his eyes open and saw Silverthorn standing in front of him once more. He did his best to compose himself, withdrawing his claws from their tacked place in the floor and standing up to maintain his noble air. However, his racing mind could no longer grasp why it was important to do so.

"Well, well," his Mistress began, "seems there's plenty to work with. I knew as soon as I saw you that I wanted to make you mine."

"Yes, Mistress," the once proud lion said as he awaited his next command with excited trepidation.

"I know my king values principles of mutual respect. Even insisting his subjects do not kneel to him while he's on his throne. Your Mistress is a little more strict in matters of protocol. Kneel."

Bartelmeu slid his left foot back and knelt down on his knee as his knights would to him.

"No. You are not a warrior. You belong to me." Silverthorn turned around and showed her back to the king. Her tail flicked with irritation. "From now on, when we are here and you are my servant, you will treat me as you would the Goddess' High Priestess. You will kneel on both your knees."

Bartelmeu raised his head and looked at his Mistress' back. He couldn't help but admire her features from this side of her. The narrow purple fabric of her outfit leaving little to imagination from where it met below her tail. "Yes, Mistress," he said as he slid his right leg back and brought his knee to the floor.

Silverthorn looked over her shoulder at the kneeling king then smiled. "Good." She stepped closer to the lion and looked down at him. "Your strapping body with that boyish mane and tail tuft. I truly envy your bride to be, Bartelmeu of Liborg. She can't even begin to fathom how lucky she is to marry into the bloodline of your noble kingdom."

"Thank you, Mistress."

"Yes, I imagine our forays will be few after your bed is shared with her." Silverthorn smiled at the curious look on her his face. "Especially with my teaching you how to properly pleasure a lady. But, such is the will of the gods. It just means that I will have to enjoy you every night until her arrival."

Bartelmeu was about to reply, but a small movement caught his attention. He looked at her shawl where the material intersected as it bulged up. The lion's eyes went back up to Silverthorn's and he saw a glee in them of a sort that he had not before.

"Ah, I suppose you're ready to learn why your Mistress is unsullied by the seed of any man, noble or common." Her right paw slid under the fabric on her left shoulder and pushed it down. She repeated the process with her left paw and the shawl dropped to the floor.

Bartelmeu was afraid to take his eyes off hers and see what she had revealed. He kept looking up at her as she stepped over the fabric and closer to him. Even when her paw moved to the top of his muzzle, he was reluctant to follow her guiding push downward. From her violet eyes to her small breasts with her pink nipples standing out against her white fur, past her stomach and hips until he was looking at her erect penis, jutting from its sheath with a furry scrotum tucked underneath it.

It was proportionate to the rest of her body and wouldn't have looked out of place at all if attached to a male. As soon as Silverthorn took her paw off his muzzle he looked back up at her in surprise. "What are you?"

Bartelmeu had barely finished speaking when the mouse's open palm connected with his cheek. His head canted in the direction of the force of the blow for a moment, then he straightened up. He looked up at her as he brought up his paw to rub his stinging face. No one had ever struck him before, and the shock of it combined with the situation was more than he could process.

"*I* am your Mistress," she replied with a sharp tone. "You do not speak out of turn, you do not question me."

"I—" he was cut off as her finger pressed against his lips.

"You do *not* speak out of turn. You do *not* question me." Silverthorn rolled her eyes. "You do not follow an order; you get punished. Do you understand now?"

Bartelmeu looked up at her scowl and whimpered. His heart sank again, the King of Liborg, on his knees whimpering before the small mouse.

"Do. You. Understand?" she reiterated, putting sharp emphasis in her inflection.

"Y-yes, Mistress."

"Good. Now, picking up where I left you before you were bad, I was about to teach you how to please your new wife." Silverthorn wrapped her paw around the back of the lion's head and pulled it toward her distinctly male genitals. The tip of her penis pushed against his lips and she started grinding the length on the end of his muzzle.

Bartelmeu closed his eyes as his face scrunched into a grimace. The scent of her shaft against his muzzle overtook the soft feminine one and the top layer of his aromatic oils. Soon, it flooded all of his senses, as if it surrounded him and he couldn't escape it. His stinging cheeks a stark reminder of his shame as his own arousal dribbled pre into the rug. In a dark corner of his mind, somewhere he would never consider exploring on his own; he wanted her.

Silverthorn's hips continued to grind against his muzzle as she said, "Good husbands know how to use their tongues."

The lion nodded, afraid to speak lest his Mistress lose her rhythm, but there was another task at hand. He parted his lips and pushed his feline tongue against her member.

The sharp taste of the flesh only heightened the arousal that her scent had already brought on. Silverthorn moved her hips a little faster, rubbing the underside against his rough-textured tongue. Her paws wrapped around the back of his head as she started to gyrate her hips against his face.

"Good, but you need to lick as well."

Bartelmeu murmured and then nuzzled against her, licking up her length. He heard his Mistress moan for the first time. The lion curled his lips up in happiness at giving her pleasure. That noble pride of a sovereign was being returned to him. But this time, it was as the servant and not the master.

"Now we put your whole mouth to use," the mouse said as she pulled her hips away from him. "Make sure you get me slick. You'll need it for the next part of the lesson."

Bartelmeu looked away for a moment as he considered what she meant. *My gift to you*, her words echoed in his memory. *You don't have to think*. He looked back at her and nodded. "Yes, Mistress."

"Good boy," she said as she eased the tip against his lips.

The lion was careful to keep his teeth away from her as it slid into his muzzle. She went didn't stop until his lips engulfed her. Even with his nose brushing against her well-groomed pubic tuft, he was able to accommodate all of her. Bartelmeu could feel his Mistress pulse throb against his tongue.

"Remember what I said about the licking," Silverthorn said as she combed her fingers through his mane.

Bartelmeu pushed her member up against the roof of his mouth. After a few moments getting used to the new sensation, he started making a licking motion with his tongue. The strokes were short in the confined space, but his Mistress cooed.

She moved her paws behind his rounded ears and grasped him before easing her hips back and then rocking them forward. A few slow and steady moments picked up into a more brisk pace. Her hips started bouncing with that same grace she had used while grinding against him. Every thrust, every subtle twist or shifted angle seemed rehearsed to maximize her pleasure.

Bartelmeu noticed his mouth salivating around her length. It built up to the point where he had to either let it dribble from his mouth or swallow. The young king opted for the latter choice and his Mistress moaned when he slurped it down.

"Goddess, yes," she said as she squeezed his ears. "Like that. Keep doing that."

Bartelmeu murmured a happy acknowledgment to her command. When she thrust into his mouth, he would try and swallow her deeper into his throat. The timing was awkward, but when he figured out that some softer suckling was achieving the same effect for her, he was able to keep pace. Every time she responded with a moan or a coo, Bartelmeu felt his own pleasure swell.

He wanted to continue sharing the intimate moment of submitting himself to her for the rest of the night, but she abruptly pulled out of his mouth and then held his head in place when he leaned forward to try and follow her. He whined, very much like the cub Silverthorn kept calling him.

"Good, but you've done more than enough. Treat your wife the same way when you consecrate your marriage." Silverthorn released his ears and patted the top of his head before stepping back away from him. "However, your wife will need more than your tongue."

Silverthorn moved close to him again, but a paw on his forehead stopped him from latching his muzzle on her nethers. "Eager one. That's good." Silverthorn chuckled and rubbed his cheek. "You need to pay attention to your wife's entire body. Do you enjoy your Mistress' body?"

Bartelmeu looked up from her groin, taking in the curves of her hips and waist, and then her breasts. His eyes met hers, and the authority she projected was cemented by her expression. "Yes, Mistress."

"Then show me," Silverthorn said. "I've heard your bride-to-be has a body to be envied." She chuckled and shook her head. "Though, probably lacking in some of my assets. Show appreciation for the forms the Goddess has blessed us with."

Bartelmeu looked down her body, stealing a quick glimpse of her penis once more before focusing higher. He shuffled on his knees, moving closer to her. When his muzzle was against her belly, he glanced upward.

Silverthorn chuckled and ruffled his mane. "Rub my body with your paws," she said, answering his unasked question. "Kiss it, lick it. Honor the form of the Goddess when you do."

"Yes, Mistress." Bartelmeu brushed his muzzle against her fur. Her mixed scents of feminine and masculine filled his nose. He closed his eyes and let out a shaky breath. The reluctance was fading but he still hesitated for a moment. Silverthorn's paw on the back of his head pulled him against her.

Kissing beside her bellybutton, the soft fur and flesh under it titillated him. He kissed again, and again. Bartelmeu extended his tongue and licked upward. She tasted of his bath oils mixed with the soft fur. His paws lifted and he wrapped them around her flanks.

"Good," Silverthorn said and caressed his mane. "Use those paws. Feel my body."

The king murmured in agreement as he squeezed her. They wandered around to her backside. He felt the curves against his pawpads, and his fingers cupped around her cheeks. The small mouse's rear fit in his paws. All the while, his kissing and licking grew more vigorous.

"Mmm..." Silverthorn leaned into him. "Work your way higher. Praise every inch."

Bartelmeu felt up around her tailbase, then the small of her back. In front of her, he continued upward. As he stood from his kneel, his muzzle came to her chest, then the mound of her left breast. His eyes opened and he pulled his head back.

The form and curves of it made his erection twitch. It was desire he'd never known. Her pink nipple was wreathed by the white fur. He kissed the erect peak, then gave it a lick.

He heard Silverthorn gasp and she pulled his head against her breast. The reaction elated him and he held her body close. Trailing his kisses up to her neck, his Mistress leaned her head back. As he lifted himself higher, he felt his erection brush between her legs and against her small furry sack.

Bartelmeu pulled his head back from his Mistress and looked down. His pink shaft pressing up against her while the tip of hers rested on his pubic tuft. He looked back at the mouse as his cheeks and ears heated.

Silverthorn smiled at him and rubbed his mane. It filled him with pride that he did well enough to garner encouragement. When she opened her eyes and looked at him, his pace quickened. He leaned forward, inching his muzzle close to hers.

Before his lips made contact, they bumped against her slender finger. He blinked and pulled away as she chuckled.

"I'm not your wife," she said. "That's an expression reserved for her. But, you've taken to your lessons well. Do these things I've taught you, and your union will be blessed. We give thanks to the Goddess when we love her blessed form.

"Now, I have the pleasure of teaching you how to sire your progeny. Stand up." She stepped back from the king and waited for him to rise. "I'm afraid my vows prohibit me from wholly indulging in your wife's role. You will have to learn from example."

Bartelmeu looked down at her as he cocked his eyebrow. His mind tried to wander into the possibilities once again, but he made an effort to keep his Mistress' gift at the front of his thoughts. He exhaled slowly to try and center himself, then nodded at her. "What would you have me do, Mistress?"

She smiled at his query. "Hold onto the bedpost," she said as her fingers fiddled with her bracelets for a few moments. "Wrap your paws around it and interlock your fingers as if you were at the temple altar to receive benediction."

Bartelmeu walked to the corner of his large canopy bed and did as he was instructed.

"Good. Now bend your knees, ease your body down toward the floor."

He bent down a little, flexing his knees and letting his upper body lower. When he stopped, his Mistress commanded him to go farther. He complied, lowering his upper body down, feeling his backside spread as he worked into a prostrate position for her.

"Very good," she said as she walked into his view and then leaned up onto the bed. Her paws held her two bracelets that had been clasped together to form a longer piece of gold colored rope. She folded it over his wrists and moved it around in a few loops, tying a strange knot that he'd never seen on any type of rigging. "Pull against the rope and tell me what happens, but take care not to pull too hard."

Bartelmeu moved his wrists back and the binding cinched down on him. He looked at it curiously before turning his head back to the mouse. "It tightens, Mistress."

"Indeed it does. I doubt you will have to bind your wife in this way. You'll be bound to her before the gods. Since I don't have that privilege, my bonds will have to be a little more material."

"I understand, Mistress," he said as the mouse stood up and walked out of his view again.

Bartelmeu felt her paws slide over his rear and her thumbs spread his cheeks as she had done when she had licked his backside. The sides of her feet pushed up against his as her stance widened and her penis slipped between his furred buttocks. His breathing quickened as he realized what his Mistress meant by teaching by example.

He trembled as she rubbed his backside. His studies cropped into his thoughts once more. The wilderness savages would take captive males the same as they would a female to break their will. Bartelmeu let a soft whimper escape his muzzle.

"I know," Silverthorn said as the head of her penis brushed his tailhole. "You're nervous. Your wife will be as well. Be gentle, go slow, and trust yourself.

"I'm here because the gods wanted me here. You're here because you need to be here. You have never trusted anyone entirely, have you? Completely and implicitly?" Bartelmeu's expression told her the answer, but he needed to hear it more than she did. "Be honest with your Mistress."

"No, Mistress. I have never been able to place full trust in my allies, my subjects or my advisers." Bartelmeu looked away from her and sighed. "Even the temple priests are involved in the machinations of political scheming."

"Do you trust your Mistress?" she asked and the king looked back at her again. She gave him a smile as his weary eyes seemed to search her for sincerity. "Be honest with your Mistress."

"I want to, Mistress," he answered as best he could without lying to her.

"Thank you for being truthful with me. Your Mistress will do her best to earn your complete trust in the truest way anyone can." She rocked her hips forward and the spit-slick glans of her penis slipped past his tailring. "I will earn your trust by letting you be honest with yourself."

"Ah! Mistress, it feels…"

"Your wife, if she's as pure as one of her station should be, will have some difficulty at first, too." Silverthorn caressed his backside with her paws as she held herself just inside of him. "Pay attention to this. I will teach you how to transition this pain into pleasure that is normally reserved for the gods."

"Ugh! I will try, Mistress."

Silverthorn slid her paws up his sides against his dense fur and then down his back. "Do your best to relax. You will have to reassure your wife, like I am assuring you now. If you bear with this pain for a brief moment, what follows will be divine."

"Yes, Mistress." Bartelmeu tried to steady himself once more. He focused on his combat training, how the Grandmaster taught him to breathe. Using those techniques, he was able to control himself and let his muscles relax a bit.

"Good," she said and sighed in relief. "I don't know how much longer I could have withstood you squeezing me so tightly."

"Forgive me, Mistress."

"No, there is no need to apologize. You are doing very well. You'll be chastised if you do wrong. Trust me, but most importantly, trust yourself." Silverthorn pushed her hips forward and half her length sank into Bartelmeu's depths.

His paws squeezed the bedpost as he tried to force

himself to stay relaxed. It wasn't the worst pain he had ever felt, but it was the most focused. His mind went back to his Mistress' gift once again. Pushing aside the taboo of the act and the pain, something else rose up to take its place. He could feel her pulse inside his body, just as he had inside of his mouth.

"True to myself," he whispered. "Mistress owns my body. I do not need to think; I do not need to worry." He paused for a moment as he heard her voice echo his final whisper, "Mistress knows best."

"Yes." She pushed in until her hips pressed against his toned rear. "You're a very good student. We're about to enter a realm where two connect spiritually through their pleasure. A realm forbidden to all others, where our spirits will join with that of her holiness, Pra'Lieth. The goddess of love and fertility."

Bartelmeu's chest rumbled as his manhood throbbed and leaked from its tip. Every pulse of her penis inside of him amplified his own pleasure, just as it had when she shared herself with his muzzle. The pain was still there, but it didn't matter. Nothing mattered but being where he was; where he *needed* to be.

Silverthorn pulled her hips back until her glans flare tugged against his tailring and rocked forward until she hilted in him once more. Her delicate paws continued to caress his body intimately, soothing him physically as he gave all his burdens to her to melt in the fires of passion.

The dulling pain faded away under his Mistress' touch. His mind could only focus on the pleasure of turning himself over to the unique woman that he had mistaken for a simple slave. The highest station in the kingdom was no longer his throne. It was now his bedchamber, and his bedchamber was ruled by his

Mistress.

Their lust built to a frenzy. They panted, grunted, and moaned as the mouse picked up her pace, hips slapping against his rear. She raked her small claws down the king's back and Bartelmeu yowled as his Mistress reintroduced some of the pain into their coupling.

"Mistress, this feels so good. Oh, gods!"

"Goddess," she corrected. "This is between Pra'Lieth, your Mistress, and yourself."

"Oh Goddess," he cried, "Goddess, Mistress..." Bartelmeu's voice trailed off as his eyes rolled up. "Something is happening."

Silverthorn drew her length out of the king's tailhole then slammed it back in. "I know," she said as she reached down and wrapped her paw around the base of his shaft. Her grip was tight and it made his member throb and swell. The mouse never missed a beat ramming into his backside.

Bartelmeu grunted as his whole lower body tingled. Every thrust from his Mistress intensified the feeling as his furry sack drew up. He felt Silverthorn's fingers suddenly press in behind his scrotum and against his body. His eyes went wide and he gasped sharply at the new pressure.

He roared as his body was forced into an orgasm while the mouse clamped off its escape, causing him to endure it without his seed spilling from his member. His muscles tightened as the feeling of pinpricks scattered across his loins, both inside and out.

The mouse behind him chuckled as her toy was wracked with conflicting torment and pleasure. His orgasm-tightened tailring pushed her to climax and she slammed into Bartelmeu's rear one final time as hard as she could. Jets of her seed pulsed into his body as the poor lion was coming down from his orgasm, denied the same privilege.

"That's how you're going to make the sons and daughters of the kingdom," she said as she concluded her lesson. She took pity on Bartelmeu and slowly withdrew her spent member. Her king gasped as it slipped out of his tailring and he groaned long and loud, on the verge of passing out.

She made her way around to the bedpost and loosened the knot on his bindings. As soon as it was off, Bartelmeu collapsed over the footboard. The mouse stood beside him and caressed his cheek until his eyes fluttered open and he looked at her.

"Mistress?" he said meekly.

"I'm here." Silverthorn smiled and moved her paw up to scratch behind his ear.

"Mistress, why are you the way you are?"

"It was my gift from the gods. I was born how I am. We're daughters of the Goddess. We share her love to those who need it most; trained by priestesses of Pra'Lieth."

"Who is Pra'Lieth, Mistress?"

"She is the Goddess we all honor. Mother of the first mortals and Goddess of Love. Pra'Lieth is her name in the old tongue."

"Prince Arhon said you were purchased from a brothel."

"What better place to worship the Goddess than in a temple where acts of love are expected? We trust the Goddess—and indeed, all the gods—to send us where we are needed the most. I am very happy to have been sent to you, your highness."

"Mistress?"

"No," she said soft in a soft tone. "Miss Silverthorn

will do. I will inform you when it's time for another lesson. For now, rest, your highness. Prepare yourself for tomorrow so that you may rule justly, and spread the love of the gods to all your subjects.

"Wear *your* mantle with pride. Trust in the power of yourself to hold your station. Your father was just, but you are the king. And, know that when your day is done, I will remove your burdens." Silverthorn rose and helped her king to his feet. She walked around the side of the bed with him and turned down the large quilted spread. She eased Bartelmeu into bed and tucked him in. "My gift to you, your highness."

"Thank you, Miss Silverthorn," Bartelmeu said as he let his eyes drift closed.

"Goodnight, sire." his attendant said with a knowing smile.

The tigress stepped through the doors of the Grand Hall after the herald announced her arrival. It was small, and she would not call it grand compared to the court of her father. Her long purple and white dress was proudly embroidered with Sovia's royal crest. As she made her way to the foot of the dais, the lion on the throne stood up and straightened his royal cloak.

As he stepped forward, a small mouse in a humble robe with a purple sash over her shoulder extended her paw and stopped him. Ivette watched as the mouse in a commoner's robe, wearing the royal color whispered something into his ear. The lion nodded then smiled at the princess. She curtsied as the bridegroom stepped to the edge of the dais and looked down at her.

"Princess Ivette," he said. His tone seemed genuinely happy. "First Daughter of Sovia. Rise, I beg you."

"Your highness," she greeted before glancing back at

the mouse.

"Please, my lady. From this day forward, the only ones you are subservient to in our kingdom are the gods and our subjects."

"Our subjects?" she asked as her lips curled up in disgust.

"Of course, my lady. Our positions are to serve the gods and our people. I hope, in time, you will come to understand this philosophy as I have. Now, I have been informed that the Royal Procession is prepared and the temple awaits our arrival. After our vows are exchanged, we will attend the Goddess Festival where you will be coroneted as Queen of Liborg."

"Coronation in the square and not in the Royal Palace?"

"Our subjects are eager to meet you," Bartelmeu told her as he stepped down and offered his arm.

She sighed and looped hers under his and they moved toward the door. As they walked, she saw the small mouse make her way around them, showing her back to the both of them as she padded out of the door and toward the procession. "Your highness?"

"Please, my lady. Call me Bartelmeu."

"Uh, yes. King Bartelmeu. I noticed that commoner standing beside you wearing a royal sash, and she just displayed her back to us as she left the hall. I have never seen a display quite like that."

"That is Mistress Silverthorn. She is a priestess and my most trusted adviser."

"You trust an official of the temple in your court?"

"My lady, she is the only mortal I trust. Completely and implicitly."

GOD'S PLAN
TYSON WEST

On the last Sunday of spring, at their family after worship dinner, Jephtha announced proudly to his parents, aunt and three brothers that he and Sapphira were considering marriage. His younger brothers having learned long ago the danger of exposing their thoughts in front of their parents without first ascertaining their mother's opinion sat silent and expressionless. Jephtha's parents smiled at him through their brown muzzles and nodded, not in enthusiastic approval, but with cautious consent.

His mother spoke first, "It's good that you're thinking of moving to the next stage of a young Christian's life. It is important to move in harmony with God's plan. Although she's not a fisher, but a mink, she fears and loves the Lord as much as you. Didn't her mother also home school her?"

"Yes," Jephtha nodded, "the same as you home schooled me. She graduated with me last week from Northern Mustelid Christian University. As you know we have been worshiping together, but before I told you this, I spoke with Reverend Saul who encouraged me not to announce our engagement as a certainty, but just to indicate our thoughts were moving in this direction. This will give everyone more time to consider it. Although you have met her at church, I am sure you would want to spend more time with her."

Jephtha's father cleared his throat. "By consider it, you mean to pray on it, and raise it in bible study as well, don't you?"

Jephtha nodded.

"Of course, I assume that you are not drawn to her merely because she's dark, sleek and beautiful, but because she has a pure Christian soul?"

"As I said," Jephtha chose his words carefully, "we are not engaged. We're not definitely going to get married, but we are thinking of moving in that direction. Besides, once she encouraged me to tell you, of course I had to share. Family is important to her as it is to us."

His father grunted. "Well, it is blessed that you are not jumping into this. You've learned wisely that it's best to follow the Lord's plan and will and not your own."

Jephtha glanced at his brothers. They were now cautiously nodding in lukewarm agreement.

In private they discussed her shapely legs and way of dressing that showed as much of her sleek form and shining fur, as she could, to raise fleeting thoughts impropriety in the pious. The three young fishers could do nothing but nod their heads in passive agreement.

Feeling comfortable that his parents were not

violently opposed to his intensifying his relationship with Sapphira, Jephtha waited until after dinner, when his family was going to walk in the park, to text her.

"I discussed my feelings for you with my parents. They are not opposed to us moving forward as we discussed."

She texted back. "I too spoke with my family today over dinner. Although they wish you were a mink, they feel we are closely related enough that we could form a blessed union. Lunch tomorrow?"

"Certainly."

Jephtha thought long and hard that evening about his feelings for Sapphira. He was excited by the energy of her strong body under her fur when they hugged or even held paws. He loved her musky scent. But she was proper and prim, and neither had made any physical advances towards one another, even though at times he could smell her desire. If the Lord had planned for them to engage in sexual activities, he would have them married by now.

He thought of his home schooling and how in accordance with the Lord's and his parent's plan he had first graduated from a Christian college after home schooling. Now he was working at his first job in the secular world full of sin and temptation at Clam Bank as teller and management trainee. The next step would be his forming a family. He never wanted to let his parents or Jesus down.

Before bedtime, his family met in the living room to say their evening prayers. They joined their paws in a circle.

His father led them. "Lord Jesus, we thank you for this day and ask you to keep us safe in the darkness of night. We're grateful especially for our family and the smooth life path you have given Jephtha, our oldest son. You've laid out his course in safety and security, for he has followed your teachings and love. He has learned the blessing of abstinence. He's an example of those who choose to follow your teachings and avoid tobacco, alcohol and drugs and sins of the flesh. Protect us all from sin. In Christ Jesus name, Amen."

All the family joined in the "Amen".

Jephtha went to bed, where he promptly fell into a deep sleep. However, inexplicably his consciousness rose slowly like a trout towards a flutter on the water's surface as he moved towards waking in the middle of the night.

He had been dreaming of Sapphira. She was wearing a long flowing gown. He felt pleasure in watching the movement of her body under it. He had never seen a naked female in the flesh, let alone felt or kissed one. Although Sapphira and he had kissed with closed mouths, their touching was minimal. His thoughts turned to what it would be like to feel her naked fur next to his. Suddenly he wondered too, to his great shock, what it would be like for him to wear a long flowing gown as smooth and as silky as hers and be the recipient of her agression.

He began sweating then shook his head wide awake. "No, the Devil must have put that into my mind. "

He quickly began praying over and over and over again the Lord's Prayer until he fell into fitful sleep just before the alarm went off and bright sunlight filled his bedroom. Although agitated and tired he got up and got ready for work. He put on one of his two suits, that he alternated, a white shirt and modest striped tie. After breakfast and the bus trip to the bank, found himself at 8:00 an hour before the bank opened to the public, at a meeting called by Alice Garrish, the raccoon head teller and manager. He had put his night scruples out of his mind until he noticed her sensual opal necklace's sparkle.

The necklace's glow seemed out of place on her plump neck. Greying around the muzzle, she was married to a slim raccoon five years younger. Jephtha worried about her soul. He had heard hints that she and her husband might be swingers. Jephtha tried to avoid any thoughts of such sinful activities except of course to save the sinner.

"Jephtha, you've been here the shortest time, only two weeks since you graduated from college. Our branch is being subject to a routine audit. Charlotte Crosse, a badger who works for the accounting firm that audits the bank, will be checking your work and asking questions while she checks everyone's work. She may ask you questions from time to time. I want you to answer her openly about anything she asks."

Next to Jephtha, Aaron McDonald, a rabbit in his late thirties who'd been on the job a couple of years, nodded his head. "Been there. Did that. Audits are no big deal as long as everything is in order. Poor Ralph, that hare at our northern branch, got four years when they caught him skimming to feed his gambling habit."

Susan Parson, a teller and part time loan officer, added. "Doesn't this have to do with the FDIC stress test?" She wiggled her llama ears in a way Jeptha found sexy.

Alice nodded. "Yes, this is good housekeeping. We want to be sure that our books are spic and span when the FDIC comes in here."

They heard a knock at the conference room door. Christopher Browning, a big horn sheep, who was the senior vice president in charge of this branch, entered.

He greeted everyone by name, even Jephtha, his newest employee.

"I want to make it clear that what Alice is saying in this meeting is important. Give the accountant our utmost cooperation. Now get to stations, we'll be opening in five minutes."

The tellers went to their cages. Although Jephtha was on the management training track, he had to work as a teller for six months so he could learn all the jobs at the bank.

The morning was uneventful as he processed deposits and cashed checks. Jephtha grew hungry anticipating his 1:30 lunch with Sapphira.

He approached Alice at her desk. She was talking on the phone. She glanced up at him and held up a finger.

"Yeah, Friday night sounds great. It'll be a great double date with your husband and my husband. Who knows where that's gonna lead?" Jephtha heard a loud giggle on the other end of the phone.

He was deeply curious about what was going on with Alice in spite of his realization that it might be a sin. Was his curiosity a sin as well?

"I'm leaving for lunch now."

"Fine," Alice nodded, "I can cover if we get busy. We'll see you in an hour."

Sapphira crossed the dull green linoleum floor as if she were strolling out on a red carpet. She waved to Jephtha.

Alice grinned at Jephtha. "Wow. You have a very beautiful girlfriend. You two will make some cute kits together."

Jephtha blushed. "Please. We're just taking it one day at a time with the Lord."

A broad smile appeared on Alice's muzzle. She said,

"I'm sure that the Lord will lead you where you need to go. He will surely be looking down upon you." She winked.

Jephtha with absolute seriousness responded, "I'm sure the Lord will."

As the two young Christians walked out chastely holding paws, Alice went up to Susan and laughed. "Oh, the young, so sincere and with no a clue of what their Lord has in store for them."

Jephtha sat leaving chaste space between himself and Sapphira's lean form as she carefully drove to Wendy's. He avoided looking at her legs under her short skirt.

"I'm so glad your parents are not opposed to our marrying if the Lord leads us there."

"I wouldn't say they are approving," Jephtha nodded, "but they're not disapproving. They have asked us to pray and I believe we should do some bible study over this."

"I'm not a hundred percent sure that we should wed either, nor is my family. They were not opposed to it when I told them of our thoughts, but they weren't exactly pushing it. They seemed to think dragging our paws is a good idea."

Over lunch they spoke of the weather and Jephtha's career and Sapphira's new job as a secretary for an aggressive skunk who worked for a prominent law firm. Neither of them said a word about their feelings for each other as Sapphira dropped him off. As he walked into the bank he was surprised to see sitting at his station, a wiry badger as tall as he was, with a pencil behind her ear and a notebook in front of her. She must have been a good twenty years older than he but seemed as energetic as someone his age.

She smiled cheerfully when she saw him, "Oh, you must be the young fisher who sits here."

"Yes. My name is Jephtha Asher."

"Nice to meet you. Since you're new, I was checking over to see if you'd made any significant mistakes. I'm surprised to see you've made no mistakes at all. You worry about doing everything correctly, don't you?"

"I was raised to avoid mistakes and sin at all costs." He was surprised to see she wore large gold hoop earrings. He liked her smile. He was peeved at himself as he glanced down at her strong legs beneath her knee length cotton dress.

"We hope there is not so much sinning going on here at the bank. We have the weekends and evenings for that." She winked then pulled out a thumb drive, plugged it into his computer to download data. "I'll just check this at my leisure.

"You seem to have no trouble balancing your till every night."

"I'm down to the penny, even though I understand that it's tolerable that if it's off a few dollars, it's not the end of the world."

"Ah, that's true. It would be nice if everyone were as perfect as you.

"Are you married?"

"No," he said. "But I am contemplating engagement to my intended. She and I both just graduated from Mustelid Christian College."

"Ah," Charlotte got a big grin on her face. "It might be interesting to talk to you about that. I've always wondered what it's like to be a graduate of Christian college. My youngest child is applying to colleges and was considering Mustelid Christian. Could you have lunch with me later this week so we could talk of it?"

"I don't know if that's all that proper."

"Of course it's proper. Aren't you supposed to help bring animals to Christ?"

"Yes."

She grinned, "Jesus wants us to talk and you can't say no to Jesus."

Charlotte spent considerable time at the bank the next few days. On Thursday morning she pulled Jephtha aside.

"How that lunch tomorrow? Don't worry about the money, I'll buy."

Although he felt unexpected excitement over the prospect of spending more time with Charlotte, Jephtha responded coolly out of uneasiness, "I guess so, if it's a matter of bringing your son to Christ."

"It must be in God's appointment book for us. Let's meet at the Sandwich Jungle at 1:30? Will that work?"

"Certainly."

"See you then. Sweetie!" She added cheerfully. Jephtha felt a not unpleasant surprise for a moment then as he thought about what she called him, he fell back to uneasiness over the danger of sin. Then, he recalled Alice had asked him to cooperate with Charlotte.

The next day at 1:30, he walked in to the bright sandwich shop and saw Charlotte drinking an iced tea texting on her cell phone. She was dressed in a skirt that came above her knees and with a low cut blouse sitting in a corner booth.

She waved to him. He could not take his eyes off her legs and clevage. For a female her age she was trim and fit. Her fur did not have the sheen of Sapphira's uniform dark coat, but its patterns of brown and grey were pleasurable to look at. His lack of will power piqued him.

After they ordered, and she grinned, "What was it like going to a Christian school?"

"We learned about the Lord, and we studied mathematics, and the usual subjects. There's no evolution though in biology, but we take classes on creationism."

"So they are sure that badgers, minks, weasels, fishers and others were just made that way in the beginning?'

"That's what the bible says."

She smirked and changed the subject, "Do they monitor your life there?"

"What do you mean 'monitor my life'?"

"Were there curfews?"

"Yes."

"Were there co-ed dorms?"

"No," he said. "Men and women are strictly segregated. In fact they were very careful about our dating. They discouraged us from dating other species."

"So you're a virgin, huh?"

"Yes." Jephtha was taken aback. "Why would you be asking me a question like that?"

"I'm just curious. I want to make sure my son is in the proper environment. I wouldn't want him exposed to anything that might hurt his chance at salvation."

"Wouldn't be more appropriate if I spoke with your son about this?"

"It might be, but I can help carry the message a lot better. I'm curious. How did you learn about sex?"

"They taught us in Sunday School. They told us what it's like and the diseases we could catch and how to be careful not to do it."

"Do they tell you that a man is supposed to be the aggressor as far as sex is concerned?"

"By the aggressor, do you mean a man is supposed to

instigate physical contact with a woman?"

"You could say that. Have you ever instigated any physical contact with your fiancée to be?"

"We've kissed chastely and held hands, but we've never taken our clothes off nor have I felt her naked fur if that's what you mean."

"Do you think it might be natural that you might take your clothes off? Maybe the Lord made our fur to meet with other fur without any cloth between?"

"In the right circumstance when we are married in the eyes of God then that would be God's expectation."

"Don't you think there's something else out there that binds us besides just the Lord? Don't you think that sexuality bonds a couple and leads to greater intimacy? Intimacy leads to trust then to a deeper understanding of ourselves and our souls."

"Yes, I can see that!" Jephtha was shocked as he suddenly realized how he had been lead into this conversation. Charlotte, a perfect stranger, smoothly and naturally moved him through the stone walls of his guarded neurosis which he saw as a spiritual shield holding off the Devil's sweet temptations. He was not offended at her questions. She had asked them so sweetly and gently that he never realized he should feel uncomfortable. Even as it hit him that the Devil through her could be leading him down the path of sin, he could not stop pouring out his soul to this slightly wrinkled and greying but very attractive and lively badger.

"I'm wondering why Sapphira does not hold me and respond to my touch."

"Do you think she's waiting for you to make the first move beyond hand holding? Or is she going through the motions of what is expected of her?"

"The Bible teaches us that the man is the head of the

household and must be strong. I've tried several times to hold her. I put my paws on her knees and she pushes them away. I put my arms around her and she may not push me away from a little light hugging, but nothing more. I've attempted to kiss her at length, but she turns her muzzle away after a few seconds."

"Do you think she likes you?"

"What does like have to do with love?" Jephtha mused. "If you love someone, you don't need to like them."

"Honey, if you want to have a relationship that works for little longer than a few rolls in the hay, it's better to like your partner than it is to love them. I'll tell you what, it's Friday night tonight and I'll betcha you and she are going to be seeing each other this weekend."

"Yes. We have a date for tomorrow night to attend the cinema."

"No doubt to see a good PG thriller."

"No. We're planning on seeing *The Scent Book*."

"I have an idea, maybe she's expecting you to be more dominant. Try it and see."

Jephtha was torn and troubled.

"Thank you for lunch," he smiled meekly.

She held out her paw and he reached to shake it, but she did not let him go right away.

"You're one confused young fisher. Somebody needs to teach you what it means to be an adult."

"I have Reverend Dellens and Jesus for that."

"All they can teach you is what's in the book. There's a lot more in the world than is in one book, no matter how popular that book may be. There is truth in fur, flesh and feelings. I like you and I have enjoyed talking with you. Here is my number. Call me if you need some coaching after your date with Sapphira."

Jephtha nodded and smiled, surprised that her

concern seemed so natural.

Jephtha went back to the paper and computer screen reality at his teller's cage, even as he kept coming back to images in his mind of Charlotte's breasts and her legs. For being as old as she was, Charlotte was in very good shape. Then it hit him. Her body was not so prim and perfect and sleek as Sapphira's but seemed far more welcoming. He realized he should firm up his date with his intended. On break he texted Sapphira, and they agreed to where they were going to have dinner before the movie.

That night, as he tried to fall asleep, Jephtha kept thinking over and over again about whether he should be more assertive. He prayed about it. At 3:00 am he woke up and decided Jesus wanted him to study the bible. He blinked as he turned on the lamp by his bed. He turned to Genesis where he read up on Jacob laboring for seven years and was tricked into marrying Leah initially rather than Rachel. Even though mustelids are God's chosen species who saw God the father as a grey haired wolverine, fishers suffered more social and job discrimination than minks. Maybe, Sapphira deep down resented the fact she was involved with a fisher.

That Saturday night, Jephtha borrowed his father's car and stopped at Sapphira's house to pick her up. As he went inside he was surprised to see Sapphira's father sitting in his easy chair drinking a cold beer.

"Would you like one?"

"No. Thank you, Sir," Jephtha nodded trying to seem nonchalant.

Sapphira's mother, Ruth, came out and smiled weakly.

"Welcome. It's good to see you again. How's your job at the bank?"

"We have had an auditor there most of the week. I guess that is not all that unusual in the banking business."

Her eyes darkened slightly. "No. If an auditor is there that long, something must be awry. I worked at the credit union for many years and auditors are usually looking for is embezzlement. Be sure you double check your till to make sure make no mistakes."

"They say I'm the most accurate there," Jephtha was suddenly uneasy. Had Charlotte been setting him up?

As he looked up Sapphira flowed into the room. She had on a blue velvet low cut and sleeveless dress. As it was warm out, its skirt circled around her just above her knees over her white open toed sandals. She smiled coldly at Jephtha.

"My parents are most pleased that we are going out together. They know you're a good Christian."

"I try to walk in the way of the Lord."

Jephtha saw Ruth nodding righteously, then caught Sapphira's father, suppressing a chuckle.

"Well, daughter," Ruth said, "have a chaste but nice date."

As Ruth turned, Jephtha caught her dad giving him a big wink.

Jephtha walked Sapphira to the car, and opened the passenger door for her averting his eyes as her dress rode up on her thighs as she slid in and sat down.

She sat primly beside him, and did not snuggle up close to him. She smiled cooly during their mostly quiet ride to the restaurant.

At dinner she served up small talk. Jephtha asked about her week and only got a response of any substance from her when he brought the subject to possible marriage.

"My father would certainly like to see me wed. That means I would be out of the house, and he would have a little less chaos under his roof. My brother and my sister have already moved on and I, being the youngest, am the last at home."

Jephtha reached over to put his pads on top of Sapphira's, bejeweled paw. She let him place it there for a few seconds then pulled away. Jephtha dutifully paid and left an appropriate tip then they went to see *The Scent Book*, "a real chick flick", as his brothers called it.

At the movie as the lights dimmed, he put his arm around her, and began rubbing the smooth bare fur on her arm.

She shifted to get his arm off her. He reached over and held her paw, but this time she held him back. It seemed as though she was thinking, that it was a lot safer to keep his paw in hers than let it roam free.

"If I'm to be a husband," Jephtha kept thinking, "I must be assertive; I must be a male." He felt uneasy as he tried to get more intimate with her. The idea of his asserting himself seemed a bit disdainful. Eventually he and Sapphira reached the angle of repose. He pushed hard enough to touch her bare fur so he felt they shared a special bond. She gave enough to hold his attention but not compromise her principles. Jephtha's mind flitted back to the story on the screen about a weasel couple's tumultuous courtship. He really liked the way the leading lady's nipples brushed against her red silk blouse. These feelings did not stop him from wondering who he would look and feel if he could wear that blouse.

After the movie and his and Sapphira's tears over its sad end, they parked at a look out over the city next to a couple of other cars nearby.

"I am the male," he worried in his soul, "and the Bible commands to act like one. Yet why do I want to wear bright soft clothing? Is the Devil in my head?"

If he could go further with Sapphira, he was sure that the temptation of wishing to dress like a female would leave. He put his arm around Saphhira's round shoulder. He kissed her and pushed his tongue between her lips. She pushed his tongue out with hers, and slid his paw down along her arm to her paw where she could grab it. Jephtha slipped out of her trap and on the outside of her clothes touched her breast.

She froze. Feeling suddenly uneasy and guilty Jephtha froze too. He moved away his paw away. Sapphira relaxed.

"I'm not trying to be sinful," Jephtha announced." "I'm trying to follow the path of the Lord. I believe he wants me to hold you."

"Are you sure that's not the Devil speaking in your head?"

"It feels mildly pleasurable, but I'm uneasy. We need to follow God's plan for us."

"What if my fur starts getting wet and sticky?"

"How far do you think we should go?" He asked.

"I'm scared," she said. "Not just for fear of pregnancy, but for fear of making Jesus cry. Do you love me?"

"I believe I love you, Sapphira."

"I believe I love you, too, Jephtha."

"But do you like me?"

"I'm not sure about that. I mean you're a God fearing young mustelid, but I never thought of myself as liking you. You're the next step in what my parents expect me to become."

Jephtha being this close to her, he could already feel his fur getting wet and member getting hard.

He was frustrated, but because he'd never masturbated, sex and the idea of sex to him was feeling unfulfilled.

"Don't do anything that would make you ashamed," he heard his mother's words. If he pushed ahead with touching Sapphira's naked fur, he would undoubtedly feel shame. That shame, however, was less than the shame he felt for his desire to dress like a female.

"What are we to do? We're not really engaged," Jephtha muttered.

"We need to spend more time together to see if this is part of God's plan. Perhaps he has another destiny for each of us. I asked my mother about love. She said she could not define it, that I would know it once I found it. Let's go."

Jephtha drove her home and then kissed with a brief and chaste peck, under the porch light.

"I think I love you," she held his paw for a second, "And I think you love me."

"I know I love you," he said squeezing her paw. Then he reached around and held her behind in his other paw. She quickly twisted free and patted his paw with hers then went into the house.

Jephtha walked back to his car very slowly, feeling ashamed, frustrated and angry all at once.

He was supposed to want her. But most of his attempts at biblical masculinity frustrated him. He was feeling a forbidden desire of wanting to be like her or what a female is supposed to be -- soft, open, desirable, ready to receive and above all submissive. He couldn't sleep as images of what he would feel like with bright colored and soft clothes wrapping his muscular brown body.

Finally, in the wee hours of the morning he fell into a

fitful sleep. The desire to be a good and God fearing son pinned him like a bug to a mat but it could not drive out the feelings of what wearing a flimsy pink dress and a bra and panties might feel like out of his mind.

Maybe they should skip the engagement and just get married. Or maybe, just maybe, he thought, he should go out to lunch with Charlotte again.

He saw Sapphira at church and they greeted as if their date the night before had been perfect. Each spent Sunday with their own family. When he got to work on Monday, he was nervous. He had in retrospect a horrible weekend. But now his concern rose up like Samuel's ghost from the earth if there were an issue at work with his till. Alice called him in to her office.

"You were twenty dollars short on Friday."

"I was?"

"We think we found the mistake. We watched the video tapes, you gave too much money to the cute chipmunk cashing her paycheck."

"I apologize, I'll pay for my mistake."

"Well, you're within the tolerances for the week. That was an unusual amount for one day. But since you were perfect the rest of the week it all balanced out. You seemed distracted Friday after lunch and you seem even more upset now."

"I apologize, I'll do better."

"Is something bothering you?"

"Nothing I can talk about here."

"Take care," Alice smiled. "Charlotte says you seem like a nice young fisher."

"I try. I hope the Lord makes me thus."

He tried to set up a lunch with Sapphira that week. That she put him off again and again with cool and sweet excuses. Charlotte came to the bank late Thursday afternoon. After visiting with Alice she called Jephtha into the conference room to meet with him alone.

"Alice tells me you seem out of sorts this week. Are you upset about the shortage on Friday?"

"No."

Charlotte came up and put her arms around him. "When I see you suffer like this makes me feel sad."

"I'm having trouble with Sapphira."

"Maybe we should go out on a friend date. You and I can go to dinner and talk over what is going on. You're almost like a son to me. I'll meet you at the Song Hay restaurant at 6:30 tomorrow. We'll have dinner in the bar. Nobody who knows you, I'm sure, will see you there."

Jephtha was surprised at how quickly and eagerly he accepted.

That Friday he dutifully met Charlotte. As he drank Coca Cola and she sipped a glass of rosé, spilled his guts on the formica booth table in a smelly deserted bar that had seen better days.

"I don't know if she likes me. She says she loves me, but she doesn't say she likes me."

He described his frustrating attempts at increasing their intimacy. In the dim light, he couldn't see the flicker in Charlotte's eyes. After dinner, Charlotte turned to him and took him by the paw.

"Would you like a glass of wine?"

"No, it's not right."

"Have you had wine before?"

"Yes, it's not forbidden in the church. But I fear it would distract me from the Lord.'

"Does it have a bad effect on you?"

"No."

"Well, maybe you should drink Christ's tears right now and see what they do for you. They have lacryma cristi here. "

"Okay, I'll have one glass of the lacryma cristi."

Charlotte motioned to the bartender. "I guess we'll have dinner here and my companion will have a glass of that special white wine."

The bartender turned to Charlotte and smiled. "I suppose I don't need to ask him for an ID do I?"

"No," Charlotte grinned. "He's 22. More than old enough to be legal."

The bartender, a red panda, shrugged his shoulders. He took their order and brought Jephtha a glass of the dry white wine from grapes grown on the slopes of Mt. Vesuvius.

Charlotte stared at him smiling warmly. I am simply going to ask you questions. You don't need to answer them out loud if you don't want to. I want you to think.

"You've been out in the real world in a non-Christian environment for less than two months?"

"Yes."

"Has the view you've got of the world changed at all since you started work?"

"Yes. I see that there are a lot of dishonest people. That's why we are so untrusting at the bank."

"Do you think that might be why business is structured the way it is, people concerned about people taking shortcuts?"

"Yes. I can see that."

"And have you really experienced the shock that people live and believe different things than you do?"

"I'm beginning to get that. But I also learned that last year when I went on a mission for the summer before my last year of college. We went to a town in Mexico where

117

I was astonished to see the drug trade and prostitution taking place."

"You ran into a Catholic culture there, didn't you?"

"Yes. And I also ran into Santa Muerte, and what my minister said was the Mexican folk religion. They don't even believe in Christ, but what I later learned was the resurrected Aztec god of the dead."

"Did you find these things shocking?"

"No. It just expanded my view of things."

"So let's get back to Sapphira for minute." Charlotte raised her finger. "Is she as experience with the world as you are?"

Jephtha thought for moment. "No. I'm her first real boyfriend, and she wasn't even on a mission. Her family was afraid she might get kidnapped or hijacked by some false ideology."

"Okay," Charlotte whispered. "Do you think maybe each of your families is pushing you in this direction with each other, not because the two of you particularly want to go there, but because they want you safely out the house and because as young people you want to belong and you see your friends getting married? Belonging at your age means the time has come to take the next step in growing up."

"Let me tell you about myself."

The waiter had returned, with the food. Charlotte finished her wine and ordered an iced tea. After the waiter set the food on the table, Charlotte pulled out the chopsticks to eat.

Jephtha picked up a fork and Charlotte smiled.

"Why don't you try using the chopsticks?"

"Because I don't know how."

"What if I teach you?"

"Okay."

Charlotte stood up and came around to his side of the table, picked up the chopsticks, and put them in Jephtha's paw. She showed him how to position them and two or three different ways of holding them.

"If you do it this way," she pointed out, "you can even pick up a grain of rice. Although, most of the rice with this type of food sticks to itself so you can pick it up in clumps."

Jephtha found himself relaxing more and more. Not only from the effect of the wine, but also from Charlotte's kindliness and her expanding his world.

Charlotte sat down again, and between bites, told her story. She had gone to church in her youth, but never been involved in religion so deeply as Jephtha. She had taken math classes in high school that excited her and took more in college. Eventually she met her future husband, a civil engineer, in college. They had married and had two children, and he, a badger himself, he was more concerned about maintaining control as he worked for the state designing roads. After her kids started back to school, Charlotte went back completed her college degree in accounting. She wanted to become a CPA, not just a bookkeeper, but her husband opposed it.

She wiped her muzzle with her napkin, and sat back and looked at Jephtha.

"That's really good moo shu pork.

"Unfortunately, the break came between my husband and I over work. Strange as it sounds, it was not a question of him not me wanting to make the extra money, but my becoming more assertive as I realized I could take care of myself. Do you think that one of the reasons way Sapphira is at least paying lip service to the idea of marrying you is because she can't take care of herself?"

Jephtha stared and looked for a second. "Why....?"

"What is she doing for a job right now?"

"She's working in a Christian day care with children."

"And you are working at the bank as a management trainee? That means you will be getting a real job someday."

"Yes. I hope to be a manager so I can support her and our kits."

Charlotte leaned back in her chair. "I think I'll have one more glass of wine and then you and I are going to walk at Cliff Park. I always find looking down on the city from a high place helpful to give perspective."

About a half hour away from the Song Hay, Cliff Park held a large basalt mound with a three foot high stone wall around its perimeter. The steps going up to it were a bit rough and risky but the top had a great view of the city at night through the ponderosa pine trees.

The flat grassy area at the top was popular with couples at night. As tall as it sat, an excellent view of the entire city from the river spread out to the north.

"We'll leave your car here in the parking lot," Charlotte said, "and then I can bring you back here when we're done. Do you want another glass of wine, after all I'm driving?"

"I'm starting to feel a little upset with this talk."

Charlotte winked, "Well, if you weren't a little upset I'd be really worried about you."

"Okay. I'm with you." Jephtha hesitated for a moment. Where was this badger leading him? She might be leading him to a better understanding of where he was going or into greater sin.

"Yes, I'll have another glass of wine, then let's go."

Charlotte nodded to the red panda behind the bar

for another glass of lacryma christi.

Charlotte and Jephtha climbed together holding paws, on the rough stone steps cut from basalt. At the top, Jephtha, emboldened by the tears of Christ, got behind her and wrapped his arms around her. Their heads touched side by side. They stared open endedly at the city lights and the cars going up and down the main streets of the city. As the traffic lights looped on and off in the distance from green to yellow to red. Neither spoke.

Suddenly she turned and pulled him against her face to face then wrapped her arms around him.

He felt immensely comforted and hugged her back.

She placed her muzzle against his and began kissing him softly not attempting to get passionate. Jephtha kissed back keeping his muzzle shut and fighting the urge to thrust his tongue between her lips. Suddenly she reached down between his legs, and found his hard member and held it in her paw.

Shocked at first, he did not move. He wanted her to keep holding him. "That feels so good," he whispered.

Then he thought about Jesus then thought about Sapphira and tried to pull away but without much resolve.

Charlotte just pulled him in tighter and reached her paw around member and held it tighter.

She whispered, "I could say here and now, that if you want the gift of knowledge, you can fall down and worship me. I believe that your savior had the same opportunity but declined. I am guessing you will accept. You need this."

"I like this. I feel good with you."

"You're a little upset right now. I want to upset you to teach you. I'm thinking that we are both moving in the same direction. I just hope the lessons don't move faster than we both can control. How do you feel about me?"

"I like you."

"I like you. I am not trying to break you and Sapphira up. I am sorry we got a little too intimate a little too fast tonight. Let's stay friends and just keep talking. I want you to go as far with Sapphira as, you would say, 'The Lord leads you in accordance with his grand plan.'" She released her grip.

They walked down the stone steps holding paws. She drove Jephtha back to his car, in the Song Hay parking lot, and by now, his head had cleared of the wine but not his desire to hold Charlotte fur to fur. His confusion started coming back about what he really wanted. He liked Charlotte's aggressiveness.

They shook hands goodbye and he drove home and got into bed. He could not sleep after an hour of tossing. He called Charlotte.

"I am sorry to call so late."

"That's okay, I was thinking about you. You are a crazy mixed up kid," she giggled sweetly.

"Charlotte, I would very much like to fall down and worship you."

"You may get your chance, but you may get a lot more that you bargained for. I honestly had been thinking we may get intimate at some point. But now that I sense your desire to submit and I have discovered my desire to discipline, I have no ability to plan anything about us." This confession confused Jephtha.

They talked for a couple hours in what seemed like a few minutes and reluctantly said goodbye.

The next morning, Jephtha got up surprised as how refreshed he felt after so little sleep. He felt a gush of guilt. Charlotte was a few years older than his mother. He had been thinking thoughts about Charlotte he should reserve for Sapphira. He texted Sapphira to see if she wanted to go to ice cream.

She replied, "Yes, we need to talk. Let's meet at Bethany's Ice Cream Palace at 1:30."

He did his chores around the house, and cut the yard, then showered and drove to meet Sapphira.

Sapphira sat with a neutral expression in a booth. She wore a pure white flowing cotton dress up to neck, with long sleeves and a hem that fell to her ankles. They made small talk until they got cones in their paws when Sapphira suddenly got serious. "I was trying to call you last night," she smiled as she took a big lick on her cold vanilla cone.

Jephtha took a spoonful out of his spumoni, and muttered. "I like spumoni. It gives you several different flavors."

"I like vanilla. You always know what you're going to get. So tell me, last night I tried to call you to see how you were doing. I was thinking we could have ice cream today."

"Well we did, didn't we?"

"But you weren't around," she smirked. "Where were you?"

"My phone was off."

"I drove by your house and your car was not there. Where were you?"

"I was out with a friend."

"What friend?" Sapphira honed in to him.

"Charlotte, who is trying to help me understand my feelings."

"And who is this Charlotte?"

"She's the auditor at the bank. She works for an

accounting firm. She's an older lady."

"And did you touch her, did you kiss her, and did she kiss you?"

Jephtha could not lie. "I must tell the truth, we did have dinner and we did walk together but I never had sex with her. She did touch me with her paws."

"And where did she touch you?"

Jephtha was frightened, upset and guilty at his betrayal of Sapphira and her trust, but as he looked into her eyes, he was shocked to see Sapphira was not angry. Her eyes were smiling. He felt another feeling he had never felt before. He was going to protect Charlotte.

"I, of course," Sapphira jumped in before he could speak, "knowing that you've gone this far, and not pushing you to confess the full length of your sin, must break off our approach towards engagement. You are a sinner. And your paws shall never touch my fur again."

Jephtha was shaking. "Please, I'm trying to do the right thing. It seems like you're my intended, that God intends us to be together."

"Did God intend you to commit adultery with that woman?"

"We didn't commit adultery."

Silently Sapphira neatly sat back and watched him. She slowly licked her ice cream cone in a most sensual way, ate the waffle cone savoring each bite and delicately wiped her muzzle. She looked up, "I'm afraid this concludes things between us. You're not a bad person, but clearly the wages of sin is death – the death of our engagement. You are now paid in full."

She stood up, walked out to her car alone after indicating to Jephtha that he was to stay in the booth as she left. She got into her car and calmly drove away. Jephtha was relieved. He did not have to stage a protest and beg forgiveness. Jephtha took his phone out and immediately called Reverend Saul. His parents would need an explanation. As close as they were to Reverend Saul, Jephtha, calculated he could help manage the bad news. He confessed to him what had happened, of course not telling more than he and Charlotte held paws.

"I can talk to you in person later this week," Reverend Saul responded. "It's clear to me that you've followed the easy path of sin. You should not have thought of another woman while you were involved with so fine a young mink as Sapphira. You must atone for your sins. You must atone for even feeling the way you do. Call me on Wednesday."

Jephtha was shaking. His life was about to explode. His parents would question him endlessly. If Reverend Saul would not talk and Sapphira cut him loose, Charlotte was his only hope. He texted her. "Sapphira broke it off with me. Can we talk?"

His phone rang. "Darling," Charlotte spoke. "Where are you?"

"I'm a few blocks away from Lincoln Park."

"Fine. Meet me under the statute there."

He drove to Lincoln Park, his mind boiling with the idea that he was a sinner.

He had lost Sapphira. She, as a Christian, should have forgiven him and broken up after much talk. Sapphira seemed too eager to jump on his mild confession. Did he lose her because of his strange ideas, the thoughts that he never articulated to her but she could somehow sense, that he wanted her to humiliate him, that he wanted to be her slave dressed in pink lace?

About a half an hour later Charlotte pulled up at the park.

"Hop in. Let's go have something to drink."

"Where are we going?"

"My house."

As they drove the winding road past mobile homes on acreage with garages that held 4x4 pickups then past an old cemetery poorly tended that ran up a hill with hundreds of lilac bushes, Jephtha's mind flitted past images of couples who bond and find their own warms pools of light in the darkness and the opacity of death itself. Death was that solid veil that every cleric of each religion is sure he or she can see through clearly. Nothing was clear now to Jephtha except his trust in Charlotte. He confessed to her very slowly of his pain and his shame and the breakup up and his futile call to the Reverend Saul and his desire to not be the aggressor in sex.

"It looks like," she chuckled sweetly, "the whole world is conspiring, even the ones who profess to love, to turn you into a sinner."

Jephtha shook his head, "I don't know what's going on. I'm so confused."

"Well, maybe that's the problem with being so religious, have you ever thought that religion might be a way of confounding young people with a set of rules that are directly contrary to their natural feelings?"

"No. I've never thought of that."

"All the nuns and priests in the Middle Ages who followed the rules never left any descendants! That leaves the rest of us who are naturally sinners, and who are the descendants of those who had sex, to take over the world."

Realizing the absurdity of this, Jephtha laughed.

"You keep bringing up things my family never talks about nor my professors at Mustelid Christian."

"It's all part of God's plan. Maybe I'm part of God's plan for you ... and you for me?"

She turned into a driveway, and they came up to an old farmhouse. Its old front porch sat above a small but well cut yard. A pole building built off to the left served as a garage. Small flower beds brightened up the simple yard.

"Welcome to my home," she smiled.

"The window in the second floor bedroom above the front door looks like a gothic arch in a cathedral."

"Yes. It's a stained glass window with a rose in it."

"I'd love to see it."

"I'll show you everything."

They got out, and she took his paw. Jephtha felt excited walking into a whole new world that felt a bit risky but not dangerous.

They entered her house holding paws. She showed him around briefly and he admired some of her older period furniture from the 1930s and the work she'd done remodeling the house.

She then sat Jephtha down at her round oak kitchen table, and pulled out a cool bottle of Riesling from the refrigerator. She poured half a water glass for him and for herself then shook her head.

"Sorry, I don't have real wine glasses. We have to deal with what we have, not what we want to have. How do you *really* feel about Sapphira breaking up with you?"

Tears started to well up in Jephtha's eyes. "No," Charlotte said. "I'm not talking about the pride or the shame or the guilt. I'm talking about the relief. You two could have gotten married, and it would have been frustrating and painful for both of you. I don't think she wanted to marry you any more than I sense you wanted to marry her. You were just going through this because of the script that had been laid out by your family. And I don't doubt that her parents wanted to get her out of the house badly, and you were a hell of a good solution. Do you know the term 'high maintenance'?"

"Yes. But I never thought of her that way." Jephtha looked up into her eyes. "I do feel relieved. How did you know?"

"You could live another eighty years. I learned one thing from being your age, and being married and divorced and raising my two children."

"What's that?"

"The best way to live is to take it one day at a time. It is okay to have plans but leave the big script to God."

She got up and stood him up and held both of his paws and looked into his face. "I've been reading *Fifty Scents of Pain*. I know you're a virgin but you are overdue for a change. I need a change and things are moving way too fast for both of us. What do we have to lose?"

"I heard *Fifty Scents of Pain* is about a strange and sinful way of looking at love. But I have no desire to dominate you," Jephtha spoke. "We are taught in church that even normal sex before marriage is a sin, let alone that weird stuff. Besides, you know my secret feelings that I told you I want to be disciplined."

"Ah," Charlotte said, "You don't know this but I have the desire to dominate. I can sense from your responses, you are willing to be my slave."

"I'm not even understanding anything about sex and I'm already moving into a strange and unfamiliar territory. Is this God's plan?"

"Are you afraid?"

"No. I want to go there and I can't think of anyone I would feel safer sojourning there with than you."

"We're both the same size we can start out slowly by

exchanging clothes."

"I've never worn women's clothes before."

"It doesn't mean to say you're gay. It just means to say you will go to a different set of feelings. I see the way you look at women's clothing. Sometimes the truth comes on to you like a blinding light on the road to Damascus. Where is cross dressing forbidden in the Bible?"

Jephtha closed his eyes for a second. "Homosexuality seems to be but cross dressing is not. I can do this. I will do this. I will see where this leads."

He began undressing himself, and Charlotte began undressing herself. They stood there naked before one another, his fur slightly damp, his member hard. She was trim for her age, but she did not look her age. He liked the way she looked. Then they traded clothes, and Jephtha put on hers and she his and he stood there in her bra and panties and soft blue cotton dress looking at her wearing his khaki pants and white long sleeved shirt.

"So much for step one. You're my boy, you're my sissy boy." The strange words felt good.

"Yes, Mistress. I'm your boy. I'm your sissy boy."

They walked into the bedroom with their arms around one another. She sat on the bed and pointed at him. "You! Kneel on the floor. You will crawl up to me."

"Yes, Mistress. I will crawl up to you."

"You will take off that dress and you will put on this pink lingerie."

"Yes, Mistress."

She pulled out fancy panties and a pink frilly teddy and he put it on eagerly. He felt softer more natural and ready to yield.

She held out her lower paws and spread her toes. "You will now lick my feet."

"Yes, Mistress. I will lick your feet."

He began running his tongue between her toes. They curled and tasted like musk. His penis hardened.

She began to moan softly.

"Does that please you Mistress?"

"Yes. Yes, sissy boy. You keep your tongue working."

He licked and felt his member growing harder. He worked his tongue methodically around each of her toes as she laid back breathing harder and harder. Suddenly she growled, "Stop, stop."

Jephtha stopped licking but rested his head on her feet inhaling their sexual scent. She had covered her paws in a musk oil.

"You will take my pants off. And then my underwear," she spoke as she stood up.

"Yes, Mistress."

She lay back on the bed and spread her legs, "You will beg to lick my pussy."

He groveled for what seemed like half an hour. "Please may I lick your pussy?"

"Say mother may I."

"Mother may I."

"Now you worm, you may lick slowly."

She lay back with her legs spread. He had never done this before and was uneasy. But he worked his tongue along her fur and it grew wetter and wetter. He had never felt this excited in all his life. Her body writhed in hard twists and turns.

She stopped him reluctantly then took off his necktie, which she had been wearing, then lifted his shirt over her head. She bound his hands loosely behind his back. With her tongue she began flickering along his crotch. She never quite touched his member but always danced to the edge of it, driving him crazy with anticipation.

Then just as she sensed he was about to come, she abruptly stopped and bent him over the bed. His naked behind lay ready for her next move.

She pulled out his belt from his jeans which she put on again. His member grew harder as she lashed his behind again and again.

"Well my little sissy boy, are you going to be good?" He was silent. The pain of each lash felt so good he could not speak only moan. He found himself relishing the pain. And she reached between his legs and grabbed his member in her hands and began tugging it softly, gently, slowly. The anticipation was driving him crazy when she suddenly held it in her mouth. Jephtha yelled out, "Oh my God. Oh my God."

They both lay together exhausted.

"I don't know what to say," he whimpered. "I feel so good and so guilty at the same time."

"We've got all night," she grinned. "Let's take a rest, and see what else I've got around here. That was a little awkward but satisfying. There are a lot more things I would like to do to you and with you."

"Yes, Mistress. I would like to pleasure you." He felt great pleasure and confusion but safer than he ever felt before. They lay together in silence and the thrill of not knowing what was going to happen next.

Finally Charlotte whispered, "What we did was just a beginning. I want to push things further. We will need a safe word."

With no hesitation Jephtha whispered, "How about 'God's Plan?'"

CENTERPIECE
MADISON "MAKYO" SCOTT-CLARY

"Hey E," Aaron mumbled, the cat nudging the turn signal lever up to make his way toward the right lane.

"Mmm?" Erin peeked up from her book to see how far they'd made it into their journey. Still about twenty minutes. She lowered her gaze once again.

"Put any more thought into the idea of a donor?"

Slinking lower into the passenger seat, Erin gave a half-hearted shrug. "Not really any more than before. Just want someone we know already and who we trust. Don't want to go to a bank."

Aaron nodded and settled back into his seat as they made their way onto the highway. "Anyone you can think of, minkypie?"

Erin caught herself about to shrug again and shook her head instead, "Only really know a few other minks out there --- the Redstones from work, and there's that

Matthew guy from your office...Matthew Lederer, was it? --- and I don't know if they swing or not. Come on, though," she laughed. "Figure out something sexier to talk about. We're supposed to be getting psyched for a night of debauchery, not figuring out sperm donor paperwork."

Erin and Aaron had been one of those couples that had been insufferably cute when dating. When they'd been friends, they'd been teased about it enough, but when it turned to romance, it all seemed a bit much.

It was the names that got most people, of course. They'd react in a few very predictable ways when they found out that the couple had homophonic names. Most folks would gush over how adorable it was, asking how they referred to each other when alone, what they'd name their children if they could have any, and so on, The rest seemed to fall into two camps: those that would ask, "doesn't that get confusing or weird in conversations?" and those that would make some lewd comment about sex, whether referring to threesomes or whether they'd ever played with another Aaron or Erin or something like that

The answers were all fairly straight forward, too, especially after several years of being asked the same questions. They would say that they called each other by their names like regular folks; they'd joke that if they had kids, they'd name them Erin and Aaron; they'd say that conversations were made easier when eye contact signaled which individual was being talked to; they'd say their sex life was private but give a wink.

Below the surface, though, were the more intimate truths. In private, they really only used each other's first initials, going by E and A respectively. They'd done the threesome thing quite a bit, actually, and even once with another Erin, it had been really rather nice, and they were looking forward to seeing her again tonight. And perhaps the most intimate truth was just how sore a subject parenthood was for the two of them, how much being an interspecies couple got in the way.

Aaron laughed and nodded. "Alright, alright," he said. "You looking forward to being a useful mink tonight, then?"

Despite all the planning and negotiation that had gone into tonight, despite all the times she'd heard it before, being called a 'useful mink' right before the first night in far too long where she really would be useful had Erin squirming in her seat, ears pinned back against her head.

The cat in the the driver's seat laughed, "I'll take that as a yes, then. Tell me what you're looking forward to most, then."

"Being...being useful."

"Mmm, so it's more the serving others than the bondage?"

Erin felt her tail start to frizz out, something she could never seem to help when agitated. A fact that Aaron was always keen to exploit. "Mmhm...mink wants to be useful more than anything."

"More than anything?" Aaron asked, risking a glance away from the road to grin at his wife. "More than the pleasure of the act, you just want others to use you to feel good?"

If his goal had been to make her flustered, Aaron was succeeding. If it had been to get her more worked up, it was also very, very much succeeding. "Yeah," she began, voice thick with embarrassment. "Yeah, I want...I want people to come away feeling fulfilled, I want to be a tool to help them feel that way." The mink thought for a moment longer before adding, "The sex is good too, you know I'll enjoy that, but being useful is what I want."

Aaron nodded. "Not to drag us back to where we were, but is that part of why you want to be a mother so badly?"

"Mmhm, at least a little part of it. It feels like the strongest, highest, and, well, purest form of being useful."

"Well, that makes sense," Aaron said with a chuckle. "So..."

"'So...' what?" Erin sat up within her seat. "What are you planning?"

"Nothing, nothing!" Unable to lift his paws from the steering wheel, the cat did his best to imply a disarming gesture with his shoulders. "Only, I was wondering, what if you got to be useful at a party like this one, and that led to a child?"

The mink in the passenger seat sat, mouth open, for a moment before finding the words to respond, "You... you're sure you're not planning anything?"

"Promise. No plans, or we'd be negotiating a hell of a lot harder."

"Well, I...I don't know." Erin realized that she was fiddling too much with her book, bending the pages, so she set her bookmark in place and slipped the paperback into her bag. "It would be a lot to process. But I'm pretty sure all of it would be good."

Aaron grinned toward the road, making his way over to the rightmost lane once more --- they were just about to the end of the freeway stint of the trip, Erin guessed, so probably just a few minutes left. "Well, alright then. So if we wind up at a party like this and there just happens to be another mink there-"

Erin cut him off with a quiet whine, her tail bristled

from base to tip and swishing against the back of the seat. "A! Come *on!*"

The cat's grin turned to a laugh. "What do you mean, 'come on'? You'd love it, you said so. You'd love to be a Centerpiece and come away with motherhood, I know you would! And you know I'm game, too."

Brushing furiously at her tail in an attempt to soothe her nerves, Erin let a stony silence fall, fighting to sort out a turbulent mixture of embarrassment, arousal, and that longing she'd always associated with her drive towards motherhood, biological imperative and otherwise.

Erin's silence and Aaron's grin lasted the next few minutes until they parked at the curb before a squat, suburban ranch house.

Aaron turned off the car and tugged up the parking break, leaning over to kiss his wife on the cheek, "Sorry if that was too far, E."

When Erin didn't respond, he reached for her paw, twining fingers with her. Looking back up to her face, he was surprised to see a bashful smile there.

"No, was just thinking," she murmured. "I *would* love that."

The cat's grin snapped back into place almost immediately, along with the start of a quiet purr. He leaned over to give another quick kiss before slipping his paw away and swinging wide the driver's side door. "Come on, then, grab the bin and let's get inside, catch up with folks."

Those who travel among the play parties, orgies, and swing groups often think of themselves as being sexually liberated.

However, they'll all be the first to admit that the time

before the play party begins can be the most awkward part. Milling around with a plastic cup of too-sweet spiked punch in one paw and a little plate of store-bought cookies in the other sometimes made it feel a little too much like a social function put on by a group of employees.

The hosts of this party, another couple that Erin and Aaron had known for a few years now, two ferrets named Elise and Joan, had set up a few things to help alleviate that feeling, though there's not much that could make it go away entirely. For every bowl of chips or plate of cookies, there was a bowl of condoms (with several different sizes present) or lube packets (silicone or water based). The cooler of drinks, normally holding just beers and sodas, also contained a few drinks made from stronger things. Small, printed signs listed the rules (play safe, wear clothes outside, and so on) near every doorway. The plans for segueing from "party" to "play" involved strip poker.

Despite all of the effort, there was still some difficulty in loosening up. This was due in no small part, Erin suspected, to anticipation for later. Even the most sexually liberated could be in the time leading up to sex.

Thankfully, as Centerpiece, she had little to worry about, in that sense. For her, the start and end to the night were clearly delineated. No strip poker for her. It would start when she was bound, gagged, and blindfolded, and it would end when she tapped out or was set loose, whichever came first. That would come soon, and the gear was all in the bin that Aaron had dragged in and set in the living room next to the neatly decked mattress that would be her spot for the night.

"First things first," Aaron said, once Erin had gotten a

drink. "Lift your chin."

Erin did as she was told, letting her husband deftly swing a collar up around her neck and fasten it in front. Although she couldn't see the collar, she knew what it looked like --- black nylon webbing with some yellow nylon woven into it to spell 'TOY' along the back and a tag saying the same in front. Feeling the weight of it around her neck, the slight constriction of her fur beneath it, Erin tensed up and swished about, her short, rounded ears canted back.

"Finish your drink, minkytoy," Aaron continued, waiting for the mink to down the rest of her soda before clipping a leash to the D-ring at her throat.

When the cat gave an experimental tug, Erin felt herself jerked forward an inch or two by the collar at back of her neck. Beyond that, though, she felt that latent arousal that had been dwelling within her the last few days finally begin to assert its presence, felt sub-space start to surround her like a warm blanket.

Her husband grinned at the obvious change and leaned in close enough to whisper to her, "Mmm, cozy there, pet?"

Ears pinned back, Erin gave a bashful nod.

"Going to be a good pet tonight?"

Nod.

"Still comfortable with this?"

Another nod, more vigorous this time.

"Going to be useful for everyone tonight, no matter what?"

Erin let out a low mewl, tucking her muzzle down toward her chest and hunching her shoulders as though she could hide her embarrassment that way. "Yes owner," she murmured, tail lashing this way and that. "Will be useful."

Aaron grinned haughtily and wound the leash around one of his paws a few times, giving another little tug to help reinforce his position over her. "Good mink. Let's go see who you're going to be useful for, then."

Erin felt like they into a feedback loop of power dynamics. The more dominant that Aaron got in showing her off to the party's other attendees, the more submissive she felt. The more submissive she acted, the more that seemed to egg Aaron on. Before long, he was encouraging her to spin and show off, to curtsey, to make small confessions to the other attendees.

This was one of the other things that Elise and Joan did to loosen up their guests. Each party --- and there were several a year --- included one guest who would be the Centerpiece. The Centerpiece had become a coveted role in the circles that attended this party, one that had to be applied for ahead of time.

And it was indeed a role to play. The Centerpiece was the one who had to start moving the atmosphere from party to play while the two ferrets tended to more mundane things such as maintaining snack levels and ensuring that the rules were followed. Once the atmosphere had shifted, the Centerpiece (almost always a known sub, but once or twice, a more dominant figure had surprised the group by serving) was to become literally that: a fixture at the center of the party, immobile. A figure to be discussed or a toy to be used in a public fashion.

Although this was Erin's first time being the Centerpiece, the role fit her naturally. Elise had leapt at the chance to feature the mink for the party. To have a willing critter who was already a well-known sub (and already quite knowledgeable in bondage) made the hostesses' jobs easier and the party more fun.

By the time they had made the rounds of the patio, Erin knew that she had done well. The timbre of the party had shifted according to plan, the curtains had been drawn, and the game of strip poker had already begun in the den. The mink was buzzing with a mixture of arousal and pleasurable embarrassment, along with a base note of that nearly primal need to please.

Which is precisely when her smirking owner and husband tugged on her leash to get her to look up, saying, "And this is Matthew. Matthew Lederer. I believe you've met."

Erin found her gaze sliding up along the slinky form before her, hidden by a half-unbuttoned dress shirt, to the soft features of the other mink. He was sleek and well groomed, whiskers bristled as if caught in the middle of searching for an intriguing scent. As everything from the earlier conversations clicked into place, she found herself tense at the end of the leash.

Another mink.

And here she was, smelling of arousal and desire: the Centerpiece, the offering to the party.

Matthew's mind seemed to be going through some similar calculation, as his gaze shifted from shock through bemusement to hunger, grinning at the slender mink-toy being presented to him by the cat, giving an appraising glance over the rims of his glasses.

Erin watched him turn to face her husband, "Good to see you here, buddy! And yeah, I believe we have." That grin widened, showing the mink's pointed teeth. "Wasn't expecting to be so lucky in my choice of toys for tonight."

Looking positively smug, Aaron tapped the tip of his wife's nose with the end of the leash, nodding. "Mmhm. Was my turn to bring the Centerpiece. Just about to go get her all trussed up. But here, stand up straighter, minkytoy."

Able only to muster a soft mewl, Erin nodded and stood up straighter, her tail flitting about erratically.

"The Centerpiece should greet all her guests while she still can. Go on."

Erin nodded and leaned in to give the other mink an embrace and a whiskery, bashful kiss to the side of his muzzle. "W-welcome..."

Matthew returned the kiss with a grin, seeming to pick up on some of Aaron's bravado. "Thank you, ah..." he reached a paw up to lift the tag on the smaller mink's collar to read it. "Thank you, toy. I'm sure I'll be most welcome indeed."

"I thought you said you didn't have anything planned," Erin said, still shivering from the mix of humiliation and arousal as she tugged her shirt off.

Aaron, already nude, looked up from where he had been rooting in the bin of bondage gear, "I didn't, E, I promise. I didn't even know he was coming until he showed up just then."

Erin nodded, anxious. She slipped shyly out of the last of her clothes and knelt, nude, on the mattress.

"Do you want me to call in Elise? We can tap out, if it's uncomfortable, or Elise can ask him to not interact with you as the Centerpiece."

The mink felt herself flush beneath her fur, whiskers bristling. "Mmnf..." she managed, then, "N-no. I mean, now I'm all curious. I've...never been with another mink before, after all."

Aaron grinned and sat down on the edge of the mattress, holding a pair of soft, locking bondage cuffs and a snap hook connector—two lobster clasps joined by a strip of nylon with a D-ring situated in the middle —for binding them together. "Oh, so you're eager, then, toy?"

Erin squirmed at the pet name. She hadn't quite left sub-space, hadn't wanted to, and so the words played readily into that. "I...maybe," she admitted, squirming tensely.

The cat's grin widened as he turned and crawled over the mattress to her, muzzle tucking in against her cheek, his paws working to fasten one of the locking cuffs around her wrist. "Toy sure *smells* eager," he breathed.

Tilting her cheek to her owner's muzzle and lifting both of her paws to offer her wrists to him, Erin whined quietly in return. "Can't help it," she mumbled, her breathing picking up.

"I imagine not." Aaron continued slipping the other cuff onto the mink's other wrist, making a show of checking the locked status of each before attaching the connector to the exposed D-rings of the cuffs, effectively locking Erin's paws together. Although cuffs were a common accessory for her, she always got a thrill out of having them put on by someone else.

"Hopefully not too obvious?" she asked.

"This is a play party, E, it's kind of expected," Aaron said. The cat's laugh made Erin lay her ears all the way back. He tugged on the strap connecting her cuffs together pulling her up onto her knees and then onto all fours, his paw pinning the snap connector to the mattress. The laugh turned into a low growl as Aaron murmured, "And besides, toy, everyone noticed." With a soft nip to her ear, he lowered his voice further to a soft purr, adding, "Everyone."

Any distance Erin had managed to gain from

the sexual dynamic to ask about plans was quickly obliterated with the firm treatment and teasing words. She quickly found herself back in that cozy submissive space, her paws clutching at the sheets of the mattress, held only as far apart as the cuffs would let them. "Was toy useful?"

Dragging the tote of gear closer, Aaron nodded, his voice muffled slightly by the fact that he couldn't hold back a purr. "Very useful. You got everyone up and moving. Lots of needy looks when we left to get ready." The cat brought up another snap connector and with an insistent push, nudged Erin's shoulders down until her chin nearly touched her paws, clipping this connector between the D-ring on her collar and the one on the first snap connector, leaving the mink with her backside hiked up and exposed. "But you're only just getting started, minkytoy. You're going to be very, very useful by night's end, aren't you?"

Erin nodded, her breathing quick and shallow in anticipation. She could smell her own arousal quite strongly, now, as well as that of Aaron, a scent she was well accustomed to. "Yes owner," she panted, breaths tinged with a whine.

There was a bit more fumbling in the bin before Aaron lay a few more items out in front of her, close enough to see but not touch. A ring-gag. A blindfold. A small remote control type device. A bowl of condoms. Two laminated signs --- one with rules, the other with a space for tallying just how the mink had been useful. A marker to go with the signs.

Kneeling before her, Aaron took the blindfold in one paw and the gag in the other and leaned in closer. The familiar scent of the cat's arousal was filling Erin's nostrils, his stiff shaft dead center in her gaze, but, again, just out of reach. The scent of him was overpowering the scent of herself, but she could feel that burning arousal in her belly, feel the cool air against her groin, caressing warm and slick flesh.

"Even that mink? Matthew?" the cat asked. It was hard for Erin to pick apart whether her owner was purring or growling, or perhaps a little bit of both. "Are you going to be a useful toy for him, too?"

Erin felt her fur bristle, that perennial reaction to humiliation no longer restricted to just her tail, but creeping up her spine to her neck and ears, heckles raising. "I will," she whimpered. "I'll be usef-*nngh!*"

She was cut off quickly. She'd been so focused on Aaron's words and the sight of her arousal in the center of her tunnel-vision that she hadn't noticed the paw with the ring gag.

With one deft movement, the cat had taken advantage of her open muzzle to slip the gag in place, wedging her muzzle open with the ring of stiff rubber. His fingers quickly traced the straps of the gag to their ends, velcro straps that looped around her collar to hold the gag in place.

"I know you will, toy," the cat growled --- and it definitely was a growl this time. A commanding, possessive, domineering growl that ensured she knew her place.

Erin could only whine and pant, huff and whimper. She nodded shakily, as much as the straps restraining her neck to her wrists would allow.

Those teasing growls continued as Aaron set up, clearly leaving the blindfold in his paw until last so that she would be forced to watch. "I wonder if toy will be able to tell it's him," he said. "By shape or by noise. Or maybe he'll lean forward and whisper to you how he's taking you. Maybe he'll just scruff the toy. I bet his teeth are sharp."

Whimper, pant, squirm. Erin couldn't manage a whole lot more, as she watched her owner set up the signs. "Please use condoms; no damage; Centerpiece will use buzzer to tap out" read one. "Cum count: In sex—In muzzle—In fur" read the other, the pen laid neatly at its base.

"Maybe it'll trigger something in you," Aaron said. He picked up the remote control and gave its single button a quick press, the small box emitting a surprisingly loud buzzing noise, annoying by design. Slipping the buzzer into Erin's paw, he leaned in closer to continue, "Maybe your body will know him by his species. Maybe you'll know what it is that you're missing out by him using a condom with you, by being that close to having his kits."

A more drawn-out whine this time, low and needy, as her owner sought out and tickled each and every one of her kinks in turn.

She was gone. Totally lost in sub-space. And he was driving her deeper and deeper.

"Press the button, toy."

Shaking, Erin fumbled with the remote, getting the button aligned under her thumb before pressing it. She got a loud buzz in response.

"Good. Don't forget that, toy." Aaron grinned and reached once more into the tote of gear. "I'll watch when I can, but I have my own fun planned tonight."

With that, Erin watched as the cat stood, making as if to open the door for everyone, letting the play of the Centerpiece begin, still murmuring, "Maybe toy will find herself needing him, hmm? Craving that mink within her, fitting so nicely like only another mink can.

Maybe some day you *will* wind up with his kits."

The cat paused and turned back, looking as if he'd just remembered something. Erin noticed the blindfold left in his paw and squirmed against the bed, knowing that the sensory deprivation would only serve to drive her deeper into Useful Mink territory.

Aaron knelt before her once more and lifted the blindfold, then set it to the side and instead lifted his other paw. In it was a safety pin, something from the emergency sewing kit in the gear tote. Holding his paws deliberately within her gaze, Aaron opened the safety pin, exposing the sharp point. With his free paw, he reached down to grab one of the wrapped condoms from the bowl.

"And who knows," he said, grinning widely as he drove the point of the pin through the package, the condom inside, and clear through out the other side of the package. "Maybe he'll get this one."

The condom dangled briefly from the safety pin directly before Erin's eyes. She watched, unable to speak even if she hadn't been gagged, as the cat slid the needle-thin pin from the condom and massaged it with his fingerpads, leaving it looking intact and unmolested. He then tossed it almost casually into the bowl of condoms, mixing them up lazily with his paw. Aaron closed the safety pin and dropped it back into the tote with a small rattle.

Realizing that she had been holding her breath, Erin let out a gasp and a shaky moan before swallowing dryly, making a soft *glk* noise with the gag in the way. She could feel Aaron hesitating, watching her for any sign that she would need to back out.

Her mind was reeling, her breath coming in ragged pants, her arousal out of control, her body coursing

146

with what felt like electricity. But she gave a slight nod of consent.

Her last sight was of Aaron grinning as he reached down to fasten the blindfold over her eyes, clipping that, too, to the collar so that it couldn't easily be removed. Sight gone, she could only rely on touch, scent, taste, sound.

The rustle of Aaron standing, the feel of the mattress shifting beneath her.

"Remember your buzzer, toy."

Footsteps.

The scent of her owner's arousal fading, the scent of her own taking over.

The sound of the door.

Traces of other scents, other people, other species, other arousals.

Voices, soft applause.

And Aaron's voice, "The Centerpiece is ready."

Short Staffed
Televassi

I stare at the curtain's stitching as I wait to start. Marie's silk curtain. My silk curtain. I try to swallow the lump in my throat, but it's stubborn.

Shadow dancing isn't my job. I'm a bartender - but when Keith 'asks', you *do*. I'm not silly enough to be the second person to show him up; no ride out of town is fast enough.

Fuck you, Marie.

I don't *really* hate her, but it helps me settle myself. It's a small victory not to swear in Russian.

If Marie hadn't vanished I wouldn't be standing here; admittedly with my stallionhood taped back and somehow crammed inside a skimpy pair of silk lingerie - *finding myself strangely liking it* - giddy with anticipation - wobbly-legged like a newborn foal.

I remembered Keith's words as he taped me up. "You

might look the part." He smirked, running his hands across my thin hips. "But even a skinny girl's shadow has no bulge down there." The fox laughed.

I thought about my parents on the other side of the ocean. If they could see me now they'd never call me a stallion again - I have to be strong and sturdy-legged, bulging muscle around every limb, but I've always kept my doubts buried. The gymnastics coaches and the party officials drilled the desire to win medals into my head. I was to beat the Americans, to showcase the USSR; a triumph for the people. I actually believed it too.

When I sat in my solitude upon the roiling Atlantic, I thought the waves lashing at my porthole were the people; the white-foam their outstretched, open jaws. I betrayed them. I had left. I pulled at my mane, I tied my tail into tight knots. I tried to forget what I'd done to escape. When loneliness replaced the guilt, I felt some sweet relief. No one on the ship spoke Russian (or wanted to speak to me), and being alone forced me to finally look back at myself. What did I want? What I'd done was taboo, but it made me shiver. Now that the adrenaline had worn off, I realised I found the taste of a man delightful.

I've been trying to figure that out for five years since. It doesn't matter that Keith forced me into this - because this, for once, feels like a step towards me, even if it is still what someone else wanted from me.

"Two minutes!" comes the warning call. I toss my mane from over my face.

My ears flick towards every minute sound; the click of the light switches, the crackle of the speakers, every time someone beyond the curtain mentioned 'girl'. If only they knew, and the thought just makes me-

My nostrils start to flare as I feel my loins swell.

I pace about, trying to find a way to make the tape not pull, but it's like being held in a pair of firm hands. I need to calm down, so I focus on my routine.

I've always envied the dancers. I'd watch them from the darkness behind the bar, haloed in the spotlight like a revelation, casting everyone under their spell of swaying hips. Back home their husbands wouldn't let them have as much as a word. It's quite something; the power to reduce people to hormonal beasts, all by one person on the stage. That's why I emigrated as soon as the wall came down - as much as I was taught to disdain the West, its focus on the individual is intoxicating.

I can be what *I* want to be.

A pulse of blood rushes through my loins again.

The red lights flicker as they warm up. A bead of sweat trickles down my flank, the heat rising as they reach full strength, casting my silhouette upon the silk screen with a sultry crimson tone. I've seen the routine before; from the other side the screen seemed so thick, but now I'm standing behind it, naked except for the lingerie, noticing the rays of light shining through the curtain's threads in the smoky air?

I feel naked - and so *alive*.

The music begins with a soft flutter; gentle, classical, unlike the tracks that'll follow. I begin, keeping my movements delicate, fluid, like Marie used to. Remembering the quiet evenings performing to my flat's peeling walls, I keep rotating my hips in a circle, arching my tail behind me like a fakir's charm as I glide across the stage, showing off my legs with long, arcing kicks. I'm going to win gold for this.

I stretch my body out, mimicking a dog's play-bow, flicking my tail around my waist as I bend my spine in an impossible arc. I was never the strongest, but I was the most flexible. I continue, trying to ignore how the silk rubbing against my captive sheath, my cock beginning to swell and throb and it strains against my panties. Every time I turn, the silk catches and rubs against me, teasing me with every move I make.

The rush of blood past my ears leaves me deaf to everything but my own heartbeat.

Dropping onto the ground, I raise one leg high, lying on my back as I twirl it about, the shadows showing a slim, dainty figure. Improvising, rolling over, wrapping my arms around my chest as if tussling with an invisible lover who bends me over, on my knees, lifting my tail, swaying-

I hear a whistle beyond the curtain -

I close my eyes, imagining a big wolf grabbing my hips firmly, growling as his pleasure dripped from his tongue. I'm dancing for him now, surrendering myself to him - and every whistle, every guttural sound, every animalistic scent only pushes me further - because - finally - I'm the center of attention. I'm no longer the slight, skinny, *girly* colt in the locker room that all the other well muscled stallions laughed at.

Now I can at least pretend the studs want me.

A loud, abrupt crackle from the speakers rips me from my dream. The lights dim as the feedback buzzes loudly, killing the mood. I can almost see my disappointment trail out of my muzzle as I sigh; a swimmer thrilled to dive deeper than ever before, wrenched back up because he has to breathe.

I lie there in the dark, imagining to my applause - it would sound like raindrops on the roof during a thunderstorm. Beyond the curtain, I hear the gentle bubble of conversation flow on by. You can drink the mood in, the anger, the laughter. I know someone else fucked up the sound, but still, I feel guilty.

This time swearing in English doesn't help.

I feel dirty, used, that I was a fool to think I could do this. A real dancer carries on. The coaches were right, as ever. Too weak, too timid - not brave enough to make it.

I smell Keith as soon as he walks in. At least he gives me a moment to steady my breathing before he starts. Just a moment though. "Get up Ruski. We're on a tight schedule. A real girl's up next." He throws a towel over me, growling as he taps his foot, coiling his red tail about like a vexed snake.

"Please don't be angry - don't kick me out - I did my best." It's the best I can come up with; at least I stifle the whiny.

"Stupid boy." He shakes his head, mane flapping softly as he flicks through a wad of bills. "I'm whatever they are," he tilts his ears towards the audience, throwing a fifty my way. He laughs as I snatch at it, enjoying nurturing a little capitalist seed as I clutch my takings against my chest. It's more than I'd ever seen back home, more than I make in a night - and the shift's not even half done.

"Even Commies love getting dollar," he grunts. "Get up kid, I don't decide to keep a new harem girl on one dance alone. Same time tomorrow filly, and bring something new - I get tired of the same thing much quicker than they do," he mutters, pausing for a moment to admire his handiwork. He grins, doubtless enjoying the power he had over me - but then again, that was nothing new. Back home it was just someone with the hammer and sickle pinned to their chest.

"Take those panties off now. You look ridiculous." He slaps my rump before walking off into the sound booth.

Even with the door shut, I can hear him shouting and cursing. At least in this case, I'm pretty sure they deserve it.

I get to my feet, keeping the towel wrapped around me, feeling self-conscious now the excitement's over. Money helps, so does the satisfaction of the dance, but they don't shake off guilt. I shouldn't get excited by wearing a smooth pair of *girl's* pants, should I?

The booth door opens. "Don't make me throw you out, filly!" Keith shouts.

Instead of risking his wrath, I quickly slip into my pair of skinny black jeans, surprised at how easily the silk slides up against the denim. Tail still crammed inside, I dart out from the stage, seeking to adjust it out there only to walk muzzle-first into a tall vixen. She has bubble-gum pink highlights to her hair, tied together in a ponytail so long it stopped just at the base of her actual tail. Evie pushes me back, pinching my arm as she starts yapping.

"Keith going to throw your useless ass out yet? Just wait till I tell him how bad that looked from out here," she says, nipping me again. Quite frankly, I let her - I don't feel anything under my thick coat, and it's not like I could do anything about her anyway. She has the first big show, after all.

"He liked my show." I reply neutrally. "Perhaps you should figure out how to make yours exciting, rather than just giving everyone a free view." I hold my tongue about the rest - she was the trailer garbage the coaches told me to mock.

"Liked? You're so cute! Did he slip you that fifty and pat you on the ass? Liked doesn't keep you kid, doesn't give them what they want," she snaps, pointing beyond the stage. "They love the real goods, not whatever... this is meant to be," she laughs poking me in the stomach.

"Evie, quit fucking around, you're on in five!" Keith's voice booms through the wall behind me.

"Fuck." She snaps, rushing off. "You fucking prick."

He barges in through the door just before I can slip away backstage.

"You're not just a dancer! Bar's rammed - get out there! Wear this and I'll turn a blind eye on tips." He snaps his teeth together, throwing a black fishnet shirt at me. "What? I don't believe for a second they're all straight out there - and I'd be an idiot to not capitalise on those new overturned sodomy laws - so get out there and give the closet queers something to get hard about," he grunts, pulling me back along the corridor pushing me out onto the floor.

There's no expense spared out here. Unlike the taped together electricals and peeling paint backstage, the lounge is covered in plush red carpets, gilded chairs, golden fixtures - all mimicking the aesthetic of an opera house - much like the stage the Bolshoi performed on back home. Round circle after circle of polished tables sit the conclaves, people in sharp suits and immaculate ties puffing cigars, draining glasses; their fingers slick between the legs of the night's company.

I find their deference to all else but pleasure intoxicating.

The smell is what hits you - a room full of the heady, potent scent of horny men - mostly. There were a couple of women too - their lighter, delicate scent a teasing glimpse among the rest. They're there likely as escorts rather than genuine spectators; their act as apparent as the bulges in the pants of the guys they tease. It doesn't stop me envying the fruit of their work though, though both parties didn't mention the truth, they still enjoyed it.

I wander through, weaving between the darkened tables attracting one or two drunken gropes from handsome men that are too far gone to register that the lithe body is in fact a guy. I brush them off gently, clutching at their fingers as they curl through my own. There's no such thing as no here, but honestly, the way I saw it, if one of them wants they can have me - it would scratch an itch I've yet been able to fulfill.

And give me more in the pocket.

By the time I make it to the bar, the swell for drinks has died; everyone has taken their seats now Evie's due to start, which means time to catch up on the glasses piled high in the sink. Keith still hasn't bothered to fix the dishwasher. 'Too much money.' Capitalist pig.

"Hey, Colt!" a snow leopard shouts, thumping her arm against the bar. I put the glass back down, letting the cigarette float about inside. "Drink." She winks, fluttering her eyes like a bird's wings as she changes tone, coiling her tail about behind her.

"Yvetta, you know I-"

"Vodka would be a start."

"Keith will be angry if he finds out you've been tapping out from the bar again."

"Do you really think so? He can hire as many Evies as he wants, he can't ever replace me."

Yvetta was the envy of every dancer. Ex-Bolshoi, emigrated or fled to the US depending on who you talk to, and either killed someone, or had someone try to kill her. The story changes every time it's told, and if you ever ask her she spins some fanciful tale about ex-KGB and a lover high up in the Kremlin. You could see it in her eyes - people were a game, and she never stopped being off stage. Why should she? With a wink and a

155

flick of her perfect white hair, she could get anyone to do what she wanted.

"When I escaped from that gulag in Siberia, I had-"

"Save me," I groan, pouring her a drink. "I'm telling Keith you snatched it when he finds out."

She downs it in one, pinging the glass back across the bar at me. I catch it just before it slides over the edge.

"Hey! I gave you what you wanted - breakages come out of my salary!"

"Please, whinny for me." She huffs. I grind my teeth, nostrils flaring. "It's so cute as you try to play stallion."

"Just take the damn bottle Yvetta and be done with it."

"Wasn't so hard! You're getting easy." She smiles, playing the femme-fatale as she flicks her hair from her forehead. But, if you look closely, you can catch it in her eyes - hurt. There's one story told about her; a wolf she fell in love with. They married, and that's when things soured. He did something to her.

"Come on Colt." She whispers gently. "You're not like the rest of them here."

I hold my tongue. *But while you may be irreplaceable, I'm not.*

The cat turns away, looking round at the latest performance. "Speaking of losing jobs, I give Evie six months before she goes."

"You think Evie is a bad dancer?"

"Don't make me call you an idiot," the leopard snorts, the fine white fur on her chest rising in indignation as she spits out a mouthful. "She's a pretty young bit of trailer trash, and as soon as she's lifted her tail for every single client here, Keith won't have any use for her." She takes another drink.

"Do you think the same of all the dancers?" I ask,

hoping to pry some nugget of information from her about my own dance. If I can get something out of her, then I might just be able to get Keith to keep me on... I feel myself stir, straining against the silk.

Yvetta shrugs, flexing her shoulders as if about to box me. She turns around, blowing bubbles into her drink with a straw (I have no idea how she got it, I didn't give her one) as she watches the show. The vixen starts her routine, a single spotlight centered on her. The light changes, shifting from blue to warmer colours; pink, orange, red, until she's panting, with each colour change another article of clothing falling to the floor...

"She dances like a whore. Heavy, laboured - just like the rest of them," Yvetta growls, turning back around to me, picking at her teeth with the cocktail stick. She meets my eyes—a rare thing that makes my neck tingle —as she flicks the stick into my chest. "Why should I tell you what I think of you?"

I don't even hear the whistling when it comes to the part where Evie's bra flies off. Or see her silk panties follow, thrown into the chest of a wolf nearby. In spite of all the clamour Yvetta keeps staring at me, a smirk flickering across her face that was full of pride - she knows, and she knows that gives her power over me.

I don't say anything. Not because the denial would rebuke her, but because there's no point to going through the pleading. Blackmail was just another way they got control, and if you didn't resist, it wasn't so bad. I learnt that lesson quickly back home. I mean, Evie knows already, so this comes as no surprise, but - *fuck* - what will she do? It's not like an overturned law suddenly makes being queer safe.

"Please, don't."

"Don't what?" She smiles again. *Zaebis*, shit, it's scary

to see it - she's being genuine.

"Do whatever it is you're thinking."

"You don't even begin to know it," she purrs, that tail again coiling about behind her. I don't know why, but it reminds me how deadly creatures covered themselves in bright colours as a warning.

Evie's routine comes to a close behind the leopard, a flourish of ones and fives fluttering about her, which she scoops up and takes off stage.

"I'm up next," Yvetta winks, melting into the next wave of orders that flood the bar. I keep mulling over her words, mixing orders as fast as my brain would allow. I winced, almost dropping two glasses, and getting one order wrong - not my fault the dog mumbled, but it didn't help me avoid a few sharp glances from my colleagues. When the rush died down as Yvetta began, I took a moment to take some deep breaths and try to calm myself.

"Martini," the wolf demands, snapping me back from my thoughts. He still has Evie's panties, tucked like a handkerchief into his jacket pocket. As I turn to make the drinks, he goes on. "I saw you talking to her a while ago," he gestures to the stage. "Terrific dancer, isn't she? Nothing quite like her here." He pulls the pants out of his pocket and testing them with his claws.

"She makes all the other girls envious," I reply.

"I bet," he says, lighting a cigarette, the orange glow gleaming as it caught the yellow tint of his eyes. "She was better than this, once."

I hold my tongue.

"Do you know her?" He continues, leaning towards me with the manner of camaraderie guys have when they fancy a girl; that sort of cajoling smirk that asks, 'help a fellow guy get some.'

"No."

He frowns, ebony brows wrinkling and creasing roughly. I can see his top lip twitch, pulling back across his teeth.

"You were talking to her just ten minutes ago."

"She wanted a drink, just like everyone else." I pause. "She was just trying to get it for free."

"And did she?" He sniffs, black snout glistening, catching the dim light as it quivered against the currents on the air.

"I'm just a bartender. I don't have much say in things around here," I shrug, hoping that'd get this guy off my back as I slide his glass towards him.

Without further comment, he slaps a note on the table, walking off before I can give change. For some reason, the note smells weird. I can't put a finger on it, but I don't have the nose to solve it. I keep an eye on him as he slips through the crowd - but a large order for a table of baying dogs forces me to take my eye off, and when I'm done, he isn't anywhere to be seen.

I was about to take off from the locker room when Keith caught catches me again by the scruff of my mane

"Where are you off to?"

"Home?" It's already half past two. "The bar's cleared and cleaned, see for yourself."

"You think I'd let you leave if it wasn't? Just because the public has fucked off doesn't mean the rooms haven't, and I've got one that wants company," the fox grunted.

"You kidding me?" I snap. My eyes are already sagging, my flanks covered in a thin sheen of dried sweat. "You never get me to do rooms, and I-"

"Don't give me crap," Keith snaps. "You know the

rules, client comes first. He asked for the skinny girly boy, and that ain't anyone but you."

"But I can't-"

"Oh come on, don't be such a wimp. Do you think they actually get to fuck you? This is a strip club, not a brothel, and I don't intend on losing this place over it." He pauses, letting go of me, shaking his head as I massage my neck. "You stand there, you pour them drinks. If they want you to sit on their lap, you sit. If they want you to strip, you strip. And if they want a collar on you, you let them - because, filly, their tips come with at least two zeros on the end of them."

I nod, regretting the silky feel of the panties I've kept on.

"Besides, I thought you'd jump at the chance of getting at a man." He pauses to light up a smoke with one hand as he fishes about in his jacket pocket with the other.

"Here's the key. Room 3. Don't keep them waiting," he mutters, pushing me forward, "or I'll see you do nothing but wash glasses."

Great.

I climb the rest of the stairs, not quickly, but not slowly either. The floors are laid with a plush red velvet, soft and delicate on my hooves, with a golden trim, and shining lamps that hang from the walls, filling the hallway with a pleasant light. The doors sit in ornate wooden frames, carved with the shapes of coiling beasts. Door number three has that of a creeping wolf slunk across the top, the vertical frames made into twisted branches and spiky leaves.

The booth is dark. I make out one silhouette, sitting upright, intently watching the performance of a thin vixen I don't recognise from behind a glass screen. From the scent, I can tell it's a he, a wolf, from downstairs, totally disinterested in the girl in front of him.

"Pour yourself a drink," he commands, waving his hand in the air in that *laissez-faire*, capitalist way.

"And you?"

"I didn't ask for anything." His tone is entirely neutral.

I fiddle behind the bar, squinting at the labels of the bottles as they clink together. None of this is anything like downstairs; they're fine wines, exquisite gins in alchemist's bottles. I pull open a bottle of whisky - 25 year Dalmore - and pour myself a healthy amount. After all, I need some courage, and he is paying for the booth after all.

"Hey, boy." The wolf pats the seat next to him. "Come, sit. Enjoy the show." He mouths, leaning back to watch the display. His amber eyes catch the drink in my hand. I can't disguise how the ice cubes rattle as I hold the glass.

"Drink up," he commands, turning to face me.

"What do you want from me?"

He smiles, leaning forward to touch my arm lightly with his paw. My heart twitched, my groin tingled. I've been thinking about this for so long, wishing-

"I'll forgive you for that question, only because it lets me cut to the matter of things. But you should know I'll be the one asking the questions." His hackles rise, even though his voice remains calm. He feels deceptive, like the flat waters of a deep lake. "What do you think of her?" he replies, pointing at the woman dancing around the pole. She's a husky-alsatian mix that was particularly 'popular' with the dogs - she looks so much like a wolf, wolves themselves being relatively few and far between.

"She's pretty," I reply, taking a mouthful. All I can

think is how I am screwing this up. How many times I'd dreamed for a wolf to show me some interest, and now that he *might* even want me to ride him, I just can't hold my nerve.

Just surrender to what you want. For once. Don't think about what others would think. My quick breath comes out like a hiss. *You're not home anymore. You can be who you want here.*

"Is that all?" he huffs, tilting his head.

I nod. His disappointment is instant.

"I want you to think carefully about what you tell me. Otherwise things will get very difficult. Tell me again. What do you think of her?"

I sigh. "I don't find her interesting at all."

The dog leers at me, resting his muzzle on his hand as he grins, biting at the nail.

"You think so?" I can hear his fur bristle against the seat's fabric, sending a shiver down my flanks, my mind running wild with the thought of that pelt doubled back against me, brushing, bucking, grinding -

"There's no effort to what she's doing, it's clear she's done the same thing a thousand times."

The wolf casts an amber eye over me, but says nothing. He holds his breath, prompting me to go on.

"I'm not that interested in the girls - I work with them, not want to fuck them," I add quickly.

The canine grins, teeth gleaming even in the dull light, his eyes catching a fragment of the glittering lights beyond. To have him hold my neck with them as he... He leans over to the side, pulling a silk tassel and thick curtains either side swing shut. Only then does he walk over and pour himself a drink.

"You can be honest with me," he shrugs, curling his tail up tightly behind him. "I'm not that *interested* in the girls either," he replies, trailing his eyes over me as I stiffen a bit in my seat. "Besides, I hear they legalised it in this state not too long ago."

"I think I know what you want for me."

The wolf pauses, cocking his head.

"No offence kid, you're not my type," he said, picking at the claw he'd been biting with another. But why bring me to a private room, ask me to drink, and draw the curtains, and do all that 'I ask the questions' act?

"If I had the time, then maybe I'd take interest in getting you to the point where you'd want to bob up and down against my knot." He huffs, reaching forward to touch me under my neck. "There's something about breaking a stallion in for the first time..." he closed his eyes, sighing. "You present an opportunity to me, however. You're staff here. The girls know you, and as you said, know you don't want to fuck them. So you are my way in."

I hold my tongue from asking why. It'd just be easier to let him explain.

"The Siberian leopard, you call her Yvetta. For whatever reason, she's decided to come close to you. It's been noted, how you talk at the bar, and it's obvious, how she looks at you. You might not be interested kid, but she's taken one in you. And you should know," he went on, snout quivering as he breathed in my scent, "she's not who she says she is."

"What I need, and need alone from you, is her passport, more specifically, something with her real name and signature on it. That's all. Do this, and I'll make sure this pony gets his reward," he sighed, sitting up against me so his groin rubs against my own.

He picks up on that with those sharp eyes, leaning back in his chair, sighing like a teacher frustrated with his students. Clearly, he expected my buy-in.

"Colt, I doubt you want to spend your life here. You know this is a lie to call it work." He stands up abruptly, opening the curtains - the husky girl's still going about her business, this time without her bra. "It'll eat you up, then spit you out soon as you're no longer pretty. Where do you think you'll go then? This is a capitalist country, you've not got the money to make it. Help me, and I'll give you a way out of this world."

With that he walks past me, curling his tail behind him.

"And if you don't, I'll make life very... unpleasant for you. You don't seriously think overturning some law means you're free overnight, do you?"

"How would I know who to give it to?"

"I said, no questions." He laughs, striding out the door, the only memory of his presence the trail of cigarette smoke he left in his wake.

At that moment Keith enters, smirking as he grabs me by the scruff of my mane, pulling the whiskey from my grasp and turfing me out of the room.

"Now you can go home," he laughs.

Honestly, I wish the wolf had just wanted to fuck me, but then I think about it. He actually has.

I stand among the midnight blues, watching as the sky began to lighten behind the halo of the bus sign. I shiver. I'm not cold, I'd known winters far worse than this - to the point where ice froze fast my mane. I'm tired - it hangs like a mist at my eyelids, tangles my tail, sucks out the spark in my fingertips.

I try to mull over what had happened, but I want to sleep. I want the 6:07 bus now. I glance at my watch. 5:19am. I groan and sit down on the curb, trying to swallow the acrid taste at the back of my throat.

I don't know what to do.

I watch as lights begin to switch on, curtains twitching. A cat drives past, placing bottles of milk down at doorsteps; poor sod must hate his job, but at least it doesn't involve stealing passports for suspicious wolves from duplicitous leopards.

A car drove by. It stops, then reverses, pulling up next to me. I open my eyes as the door pops open, seeing Yvetta curling her finger at me.

"Get in." She smiles, still looking beautiful despite the time.

So I did. She's still dressed from her last routine, which yes, involved so few clothes that it's a mistake to call her dressed at all. God, I wish I had a body like hers - thin, lithe, with taut fibres of muscle beneath. She blinks, flicking her white hair from off her face.

"You look a mess. What happened?" I hear the soft whoosh of air as she takes a sharp breath, that cute little pink button of a nose twitching softly.

"Long night." I close my eyes.

"Longer than *usual*," she replies.

"Private bar." I manage, taking a deep breath. The cool morning air feels divine after a night of humid, sweaty air.

"You're not made for this colt," Yvetta stated, her silky fur brushing against me as she leans over to buckle me in. I don't even think as I hear her sigh, the engine rumbling into life as she switches into first gear.

2:34PM

I read the time, wait for things to come back. They drip through the haze that surrounded my thoughts like water drops, reminding me of the days spent in

165

grandmare's cabin, watching as the is melted from around the window pane.

"Good morning," Yvetta smirks, handing me coffee in a pink cup with cartoon cats on it. "You were so gone last night I didn't think I'd bother to ask you for an address." I flick my ears. I've never heard her speak like this before - in the club she was always heavy, sultry. This was gentle, caring - and though it sounds endearing, it puts me on edge.

I remember the wolf last night. *'She's not who she says she is.'*

"I hope you don't mind," she mumbles, curling her tail across her lap as she sits at my feet. "I thought it was better to let you sleep," she continues, her eyes following mine as I look around her flat. It's spacious and well-fitted, the blinds drawn so I can't figure out where we were, but the smart fittings and granite counters - how could she afford them on a stripper's salary? "Besides, I thought you might like it, even." She turns away as I try to catch her gaze.

"Why?"

"I was thinking about what you asked - teaching you. And at first, I thought I shouldn't. But then I smelt it on you - that confusion, that elation." She sighs, her eyes fluttering up towards the heavens. "I remember being young, confused and excited by it all... I don't want you to make the same mistakes."

"What do you mean?"

"Maybe I'll explain," she sniffs, her nose twitching as she holds her tongue. "But I think I can teach you something."

"You don't help anyone," I retort. She has to want something from me. The wolf was right, that's how the world works. Capitalist, communist, whatever side of the wall, it was the same. It's all about people trying to get what they want at the expense of others.

"Honey, you're a cute bitch. The rest of them are just bitches," she shrugs, flicking her long white hair over her shoulder. "You're cute when you get money thrown at you," she huffs, hunching her shoulders, her usual tone kicking in.

I don't exactly know what she's proposing, but I'm not going to say no. It'll help me get what the wolf wants; maybe even shed some light on what this all is about.

"Fine," I breathe, trying to not appear too keen. Yvetta just smiles and wiggles a finger under the fluff of my chin, murmuring something in Russian that even I couldn't catch.

"Good." The leopard replies with a dangerous smirk. "Let's begin."

"I demand your respect," Yvetta commands, pulling off my shirt as she leads me into an empty, windowless room filled with mirrors. "Total obedience," she pauses, holding me back at the door. "That is what I want. You want to know one thing about me? I never give up."

I listen, looking around the room. It is strange, closeted away by a small door next to the bedroom, the walls covered with mirrors, as well as the ceiling and floor.. Though there are no windows, the daylight seems to find it's way inside. It's small, fitting the two of us just about, with enough space for me to pace about while Yvetta leans against the wall. Fitted between the gaps in the ceiling is a system of hooks and pulleys, all wound with different coloured sheets of silk that somehow manage to reach the centre without a single one getting caught up in another.

"If you will not do as I say, then I cannot teach you.

Understood?" I nod meekly. She sniffs in reply, her nose wrinkling as if my scent offends her. "We shall see." I can tell that she knows I have questions, but she flicks them away.

"What do you think makes a great dancer? Heart?" She asks, prodding my chest. "Mind?" She pokes my head. " Answer - whole body. All of you must be in motion, working together as one," she says. "In Bolshoi, you learn one single mistake breaks the performance. All people are predators, if they see weakness, they exploit it, and it's all they'll see."

She snickers, taking pleasure as she unzips my jeans and brings them down to my knees in one fluid motion. "If you want to dance well, you won't need these either," she orders, repeating the same gesture with my briefs. "You won't be wearing any of this when you're up on stage, so you won't here either."

I flinch, trying to cover myself but she just throws back her head and laughs softly.

"It's not funny!" I snap, indignant.

"But it is. You want me to teach you how to dance naked in front of a crowd, but you won't do so for me. It's not like you like girls even." She rolls her eyes, giggling.

"That's not true!" I cry, stamping my hoof.

"Then show me?"

I snort, curling my tail around my groin as I bend over, fumbling about with the clothes down by my legs.

"You must not fear their eyes, you must not fear me, you must not fear your body." She turns to the back of the room, returning with various lengths of ribbon dotted high and low from all corners. "I've seen too many dancers fail about on the stage thinking it's sexy to expose as much of themselves as they can," she continues, bringing the ribbons to my feet. "At the end of the day, we all look the same down there, and if you show it off all the time, you'll never be able to give any more. Your audience are like wolves; they love the thrill of the hunt, and so you must play the part of canny prey, taking them on a winding chase across your body until you decide it's time." As she speaks, she paces around me, tying the ribbons tightly, around my arms, my wrists, my tail.

"And this is going to help how?" I try to disguise the anxiety in my voice. She just leans forwards and gives me a kiss on the back of my neck.

"You want to know how I learnt? This is how. When you dance, I'll be watching - pulling here and there, tweaking your movements, showing you how things must be. I'm not asking you, I'm demanding you do as I say - for this is how you shall have to be with your audience, you must dance in tune with their demands," she grins, giving an experimental tug on the blue ribbon —pulling my tail up and exposing my rump.

"Hey!" I bark, but it's a pretty futile squeak if I'm honest.

"You've forgotten something," she smirks, tossing a pair of lace lingerie - complete with bra too. "You're still pretending to be a girl, after all," she shrugs, slackening my my ties so I can put them on. I can't help but feel the fur on the back of my neck prickle as I feel her watching me squeeze my sheath and balls inside the delicate fabric—smooth, soft, but so taboo. Mind you, it does make me feel *slightly* less naked, even if it is embarrassing. When it comes to the bra though, it seems Yvetta has other ideas. Coming up behind me, she snaps the ties together, making it so I couldn't slip out, even if I wanted to.

"Now," she croons, licking my ear, "doesn't that feel

better?" I feel her fingers trail delicately down my back, becoming lighter and lighter until I can't tell whether she's reached my tail or not.

"Here's the deal my girl," she commands, coming to stand beside me. She has this steely, icy glare to her, that was both fearsome and beautiful at the same time. "If you dance well, if you do your lessons well, then I'll let you free. But if you are stubborn, if you are obstinate, then I won't loosen the reins until you do - no matter how long it takes." She grins, pulling the blue ribbons round my ankles sharply, forcing me to fall forward. The other ties hold, catching me, suspending me in the air. "I'll take that as a yes," she says, chuckling to herself. I shoot Yvetta a sour look, but she just shakes her head, shushing me quietly.

"Filly, I want you to know you're safe too. Be as bold as you want, try without fear. Show me that joy you took from it that night," she smiles. "I'm here to help you."

I nod, twisting my hands round the ties on my arms as I regain my balance. Yvetta gives me a moment to clear my head, to think about how I'll go about this. I'm nervous, but I think I'll tell a story.

My dance begins slowly, gently pulling against my ties, keeping the lines taut as I move about, my arms clutched firmly against my chest, hands curled up against my heart.

I turn to the front, keeping my gaze submissive just underneath her own. Slowly, I extend an arm, curling my fingers outwards, and at the last moment, I flick my eyes up to meet hers, before snatching my hand back; flinching as if stung. And moving slowly, rising to my feet, waving my hips back and forth, I pull my hands from my heart and arms half extended, offering it up to her on open palm.

She took my cue, shaking her head as she tweaks the choreography. Pulling on my ties, she lifts my arms up above my head, and then with my left leg, makes me turn on the spot. Seeing the ribbons cross over, she grins, tying them together, doing the same for my arms and legs, leaving me hanging there, unable to struggle free.

"Yvetta..." I call her name anxiously, unable to do anything but feel the cuffs start to pull against my wrists.

"If you don't want it to hurt, let your limbs go slack," she says. "And you'd best tell me the truth." She bends down, kneeling as her head came level with my hips, her blue eyes flickering up at me with that sharp, predatory gaze.

"What did the wolf last night ask you to do?" She sniffs. I shiver when she touches me, slowly clasping my balls, lifting them up, weighing them. The claw tip on her thumb teases the back of my sack, probing the dark, leathery skin.

I hesitate, squirming against my bonds.

"Think very carefully," she cautions, letting her sharp claw-tips catch against my skin. "You're not part of this. I won't have to hurt you if you're honest."

"How can I be sure?" I can't stifle the whiny this time; it wheezes out from my lips like some pathetic songbird's call.

"You can't," she sighs. "Call it a difference of philosophy between me and him though," she pauses, giving me a gentle squeeze, "but of course, I'm here and he isn't."

I'm not exactly going to lie with a set of claws around my balls, but honestly, I don't want to either. The maternal edge to her voice echoes with my childhood, when big, strong grandmare would take me up in her arms, squeeze me tight, and tell me how she'd sort everything out.

"I didn't want to - I didn't tell him anything."

"Of course, you don't have anything he needs to know." She lets her grip slacken. "Keep going."

"He didn't say much, just that he wanted your signature - your real one, from your passport, something, whatever and that if I helped him then he'd help me."

She lets go, giggling softly.

"Oh Dima," she chuckles with a throaty purr, "you're so predictable." She drops her shoulders, letting her grip go slack as she gently strokes me tenderly, like a kitten. "He's never going to get what he wants."

"Yvetta, please, whatever it is I haven't done anything —I hadn't decided it was all so fast."

"It's okay," she whispers, coaxing my folded ears back to life. "I know you're telling the truth."

"Look, please -"

"Shhh. It's okay. You don't have to worry," she licks her lips, looking back down at my crotch. "Seems such a shame, having to keep these all hidden away."

She ignores me as I mumble something in protest - I can't remember what, but really it doesn't matter, and she knows it. My mouth's running through anything protest, but my head's already overriding it with the sensations firing up my nerves from my groin. She continues exploring, brushing my taint, gently running the tips of her claws across my flanks.

"Please..." I recall that, at least. I'm lost, trying to process everything - the main overriding thought that comes from my tingling flesh is *why*. She could have anyone, why put me in the palm of her hand?

"No need," she replies, brushing my swollen sheath.

"But you-"

"This is part of your lesson. I like rewarding honesty. Don't spoil the moment, just enjoy the feeling of me on you, and I'll tell you later." She smiles, pressing her muzzle between my legs.

I loose track of time; the clock outside the door ticking at irregular intervals. My hips twitch, trying to buck against her warm muzzle, but every time I struggle to thrust forward, she just draws back, preventing me from gaining any greater satisfaction. For that disobedience, she breaks off, licking her lips in exaggeration, leaving me hanging there in the air, the cold draught making itself known as it sweeps across my trembling length; a wet bough in the autumn breeze.

"Now, you must behave if you're going to get your release," she purrs again, tugging at my silk restraints. Her eyes are sharp and flinty; she needs this too. "You're not a stallion, by any measure," she continues, running a claw down my chest. She tuts, shaking her head as she scratches my rump and squeezes my flaring head. "You're a filly with a cock," she groans, noticing how I can't help but shiver and strain against my silk bindings in excitement. "But don't worry, I'll make sure she's well looked after," she growls, leaning forward, placing a soft kiss on my cheek.

"Please - Yvetta!"

"If you want me—"

I bite my lip as her paw tickles my sensitive flare, running her claws round the meaty rim, trailing her fingertips in circles around my tip. I'm already leaking over her, slicking her fingers, the stray drops audibly striking the floor.

No one had done this to me - no one. The loss of control, hanging there suspended in midair, it only mirrors how I feel inside - my heart fluttering away, my nerves tingling, my head light and airy. Because I've spent my days trying to hide it, trying to be someone, something else. And this, what Yvetta's doing, she's peeling back all the lies I've clothed myself in - she knows, she revels in exploring it.

"No, please, keep going." I swallow, panting. "It's just —I've never—I wanted to-"

"Don't tie your tongue for me. Confession's is over now. Let me administer absolution." She smirks, dropping her gaze to my genitals - at full mast, swollen balls, sticking out the side of a pair of silk lingerie. "I think you're adorable." She kisses me again, stepping round behind me, nostrils flaring with each breath of my heavy equine scent, rubbing her pink nose down the crook of my back.

"I need to get a better inspection of this filly," she continues, resuming her commanding tone, pulling up the base of my tail and rubbing her hand round my ring, still slick from my excitement. "What a pretty rump this girl has," she sighs, pushing her thumb against me, waiting to see if I'd give. "I think it'd be the perfect pleasure for a strapping young stallion," she continues, slipping her thumb in and out while simultaneously fondle my balls.

"Don't tell—"

"I wouldn't," she replies, planting a warm kiss underneath my tail.

My mind's racing. Yvetta keeps working deeper inside me. Whenever I blinked, I saw behind my eyelids a thick member slowly grinding itself against my entrance. I hear another splatter as another drop falls to the floor from me, my breathing ragged. I desperately want to jerk myself off, to release the pressure building in my loins, but Yvetta's continued teasing only increases my frustrations without bringing any hope of release.

The need seems like insanity. Thoughts come in short bursts, accented with sights, sounds, smells. Words start to fall away - less talk, more sighs, groans, moans - even Yvetta begins to breathe deeper, faster. I give a soft whinny as she slips another finger in, the snow leopard smirking as she tries to find my elusive limit. Then there were no more fingers, just a hunger that rose through me as she massaged my insides.

"You know..." she pauses, listening to my frantic squirming as she toys with me, "it's a myth—being able to cum just by being the bottom."

The power she has over me hit home, a wave of realisation that washes through my ragged, frazzled brain. There is no way I can release myself, her hold over me is entire. But it's beautiful, a sensual abyss I lie in, where my mistress tends to me with her feathered touch.

For the first time, I don't feel I have to hide.

"Still with me?" she purrs, still so soft and tender with her filly.

"Yes, please," is all I could muster. She kisses me again, patting me on the head as she rubs her finger inside me.

"You're wonderful," she replies. "But I don't think you'll be able to stand much more teasing." It's true, not an unkind thing. A thick haze lies over my thoughts, my brain's foggy, and each flush of pleasure brings with it an exhaustion that fails to recede.

Turning around, my mistress comes to face me again, holding my erect shaft in both her paws. She rubs the head slowly, another pulse of fluid oozing out from the tip, spreading it down across me entirely until it hangs there, glistening. Then she stands, licking her lips as she lowers me further down until my hooves just skim the floor. But instead of letting me touch it, she alters my position, until I hang parallel to the floor with the tip of my cock rather embarrassingly sliding up and down against the floor. Before I can ask, she crawls underneath me, my chest brushing against the plush fur of her back. She lifts her tail, guiding me underneath, brushing it against my groin as she uses my like a toy, rubbing my head against her heat - building the pressure, pulling me closer - until I slipped into the warmth and wetness. I become aware of my jaw hanging open, but I can't find the will to close it.

"God." I whisper.

She rocks me back and forth - the only thing halting my swing the slap of my hips against her rump. I hear her steady breathing beneath me, feeling more like a stallion. Trailing my fingers through her fur, I tickle her as she swings me back and forth, each thrust punctuated with the heavy slap of my balls against her thighs.

The haze descends. My entire body tenses. It builds in my loins, rising and rising. I hear the blood roar as it rushes past my ears.

I hear my flare pop out from inside her, and the splatter of cum onto the floor.

Spent, I fall limp, hanging there, my wrists against straining against my bindings, my shoulders burning in their sockets. But the soon it fades to numbness, creeping through my body, as if she's injected me with something.

Caught in a half-pant, half-pur, she crawls out from underneath me, lowering me down to the floor. I don't have the strength to stand - neither did she, forcing us to lie there in the bed we'd made ourselves. I think I drifted off to sleep, but when we woke I felt like some semblance of control had returned to my body, however that wonderful, relaxed sensation remained as well, sort of like that feeling after a relaxing massage.

"I should have realised earlier that this was nothing about dancing," I sigh, looking at the mirrors, the pulleys, the ribbons.

"Sorry for the deception," she shrugs. "It's not like there's much I need actually teach you, you have that talent yourself," she pauses, "and the perfect body for it too. Besides, I figure this would be a great way of saying thank you."

"I never believed the rumours about you-"

"But they were true," she sighs.

"So that guy - Dima?"

"On paper, still my husband. You don't need to know why, but I'm punishing him the way it hurts him most. How do you think I can afford this place? Every month, he magically finds his bank account drained, and trust me, I was taught by the best on how to do that without leaving a trail."

"Then how did he find you in the club?"

"Beats me. Keith's no saint, he'll sell on any information, and if you're any good at my job, you know chatter pays." She lies back against me, stroking the fur on my chest as we watch the sunset creep over the city. "You know how Keith works. As soon as Dima offers more than I'm worth to him, I'm gone. Look at how quickly he had Marie's shoes filled."

I stiffen against her. "You do realise I'm screwed now?"

"Calm down. Keith doesn't have the good fortune to know where I live, so there's time," she snorts. "Can't say the same for you, can we?" She stands, throwing me a jacket as she leads me out to the balcony. "No matter, I can sort you out so you can skip town." From up here, no one could see, so we stood there, a smirk on her face as my long dick slowly recedes, still dripping from our climax. "I'm glad you were honest in the end, kid," she puffs, watching her breath blow away on the wind. "I didn't want to think you had that kind of thing in you."

"Well, I was tempted," I confess, "but I had a feeling you'd help me better get what I want."

She flicks her ears.

"Pretty stupid thing to do," she laughs, "you don't know anything about me."

"I know you dance well."

"Bolshoi was just another lie."

"You still dance well."

She smirked at that, fumbling in her, now my, jacket for a cigarette.

"And you truly let me be me." I coughed, trying to swallow in the lump in my throat.

"I do have a thing for effeminate boys..." she said, giggling as a drop of cum splattered out from between her legs onto the concrete floor. "Seeing a guy all tied up and helpless-"

"Yvetta. I'm saying I've seen enough to take that risk. Trusting you - you could have done anything to me back then."

She dips her head, taking a puff from her now lit cigarette. She tosses it to the floor, stamping on the glowing end with her paw.

"You're caught up in this now, because of me. I knew Keith put you up to something, if only I'd smelt it sooner I would've saved you the trouble and have been long gone."

"Why don't you go to the police?"

"Honey, do you really think the US will love an ex-

KGB agent in their midst? And if you go, I wouldn't expect any help. Just because they've abolished that sodomy law doesn't mean attitudes will have changed. They'll beat you, then turn you over, because for some hating queers means more than borders."

"So then what?" I stumble, hoping that she'll articulate what I'm feeling, what I'm hoping. I silence the bit in my head that says I'm just riding the wave after the sex, but I don't believe it, I want to make this choice, take this chance.

I wait in silence, watching the last sliver of the sun slip below the horizon.

"Skip the town. And the next. Until there's somewhere we don't know the names or faces, where what we do is a dime a dozen, we're they're so short-staffed they won't ask no questions." She sighs, allowing a ghost of a smile to flicker across her white muzzle.

"And if they follow us there?"

She stares out across the balcony, across the city.

"I've always wanted to go west."

I afford myself a smile too. I chuckle, remembering the coaches. I'd been a fool to think crossing a sea would give me the freedom I craved. Here they call it money, but the power is everywhere, pushing so many people down. What irony it is, that with Yvetta I can finally escape, finally be who I know I am meant to be.

"Fuck it. Me too. Somewhere where they're so short-staffed they won't care to ask any questions."

"That's my stallion."

I can't describe how it felt when she took my hand.

Biographies

TJ Minde found the furry fandom after moving to Ohio almost ten years ago. It is there, he picked up the pen. TJ is incredible grateful for the community of artists, writers and friend he found; they helped him discover something that he cares about – writing. TJ has grown to become more passionate about the craft of writing and enjoys creating new worlds and aiding others with projects of their own.

TJ's other works may be found in Roar, Fang, and other anthologies both in and out of the fandom. For thoughts, comments and replies in 140 characters or less, he can be found on Twitter @TJMinde.

Mog Moogle has been lurking around the fandom since the early 2000's. He started writing furry stuff just for fun in 2004. Since then, he's posted several free stories on SoFurry.com and his first printed stories released in 2016.

When not doing furry stuff, he's usually trying to figure out how to do more furry stuff. He loves to travel and see new places, and really enjoys furry conventions.

Mog's had a few interesting experiences that lend to his writing, an Army veteran and former police officer with an adrenaline junkie mindset has led to more than one interesting adventure in his day.

He's usually a friendly type of critter that enjoys hugs and loves talking to readers and fellow writers. Feel free to contact him and let him know what you think of his story, (or his terrible bio.)

BanWynn Oakshadow is 54 yo hermit, writer, husband, father and Cancer. His turn-ons include sushi, long walks in the woods, interesting people that he can exploit as characters in his stories and tilting at philosophical windmills. His turn-offs are people who use bit-torrent rather than buying books, food that doesn't excite and fear of new experiences. He loves writing, but despises finding good homes for his work and is attempting to train his Border Collie to become his agent. He lives on a little 400yo farm in a forest in southern Sweden with his husband, dog and lots of mice.

MADISON SCOTT-CLARY is an author, editor, musician, and programmer. She has worked on wide-ranging projects within furry, editing for both [adjective][species] and its sister project Love - Sex - Fur, as well as Thurston Howl Publications. She is president of the Furry Writers' Guild, which strives to promote anthropomorphic fiction and its creators. She lives in Northern Colorado with her two dogs and her husband, who is also a dog.

Her writing may be found at writing.drab-makyo.com

TELEVASSI currently lives in south-east England. He is fascinated with imagining the world as other animals see it and combining it with our own human perspective – naturally leading to his participation in the Furry Fandom. Televassi writes both poetry and prose, and has a 'slight' obsession with Beowulf, The Elder Edda, Celtic La Tène culture, and Germanic cultures. Considering these interests, it is ironic that his nickname is TV. Yes, as in a television.

You can find Televassi's latest work in, Gods with Fur, Heat 13 & 14, and The Symbol of a Nation. You can also find him on Twitter regularly talking about writing, history, and rock climbing.

JONATHAN W. THURSTON is the editor-in-chief of Thurston Howl Publications. His works have appeared in Civilized Beasts, Typewriter Emergencies, Passing Through, ROAR 8, HEAT, Purrfect Tails, and more. He won the Ursa Major Award for editing the essay collection Furries Among Us. He has a Master's degree in English and is also a reporter on LGBT issues in Lansing, MI.

TYSON WEST lives in Eastern Washington with its beautiful vistas, dry dusty summers and cold winters on the bottom of the flood plain of the great Ice Age flood. He enjoys reciting his poetry to magpies and coyotes.

He has published poetry in Danse Macabre, Misfits Miscellany, Subtopian, Haiku Journal, 50 Haikus, Three Line Poetry, World Haiku Review, Cattails Haiku Journal, Big Pulp, Cowboy Poetry Press, Annapurna. He published a fiction in a vampire anthology called "You Can't Kill Me I'm Already Dead", and a steampunk story, "The Wulver", was published in Voluted Tales. He has published scifi in Fast Forward Festival and "Warlords of the Asteroid Belt". He has had two poems nominated for the Pushcart Prize. His poetry collection "Home-Canned Forbidden Fruit" is available from Gribble Press. His novella "Mall of the Damned" was published in 2014 by Red Dashboard Publishing, LLC.

Other Titles from Red Ferret Press

The House of Eros by Matthew David Campbell
Still Life Over Coffee by Robert Cone
The Goat: Building the Perfect Victim by Bill Kieffer
The Underside of the Snake by Leah Mueller
Kisses and Kickflips by Kacey Pinkerton
Knotted Vol. 1 edited by Weasel
Cuentos de Amor by Z.M. Wise